By: Cheraee C.

ANOTHER SHADY MISSION

MOCY PUBLISHING
WWW.MOCYPUBLISHING.COM

Detroit, Michigan

Another Shady Mission

ISBN 978-1-940831-04-6
Copyright © 2014 by Cheraee C.

Published by Mocy Publishing, LLC.
Website: www.mocypublishing.com
Email: info@mocypublishing.com
Phone: (313) 436-6944

BASED ON A TRUE STORY

ANOTHER SHADY MISSION

ANOTHER SHADY MISSION

BY CHERAEE C.

Dedications:

I dedicate this book first and foremost to my favorite cousin in the universe Emily R. who helped me come up with the concept of this book, the characters, and bits and pieces of the plot.

Secondly, I dedicate this book to all the shady people in the world who go around terrorizing other people's life. Y'all shadiness needs to be recognized formally and informally.

I dedicate this book to my daughter Kya and all the haters and dream killers who try to kill my inspiration and all my family and friends who believed in me and listened to my ideas with all the late nights and early mornings.

Introduction

Every saint has a past, and every sinner has a future, but for Passive Boone Mitchell and Darnell "Smoke" Mitchell everything they had and would have was a catch 22. The prominent areas in the city of Detroit were their paradise, but the dubious snakes of Detroit were their hell. The dynamic couple was still in the newlywed stages of their courthouse marriage, but nothing not even eternity was ever going to snatch them apart. Even though Passive wanted to be the first family member in her Boone family to have a real wedding, she refused to have a real wedding without her father. Every father may dread the day they have to walk their daughter down the aisle and put their daughter's life and heart in the hands of a man, but still every father is there for that moment, but Passive was denied that chance. So for Passive, she was more in love with her ring and her husband then submitting to society's typical wedding norms.

Passive who was thirty-six college credits away from being a licensed social worker, put her dream on hold for her wifely transporter duties. Smoke who was a very compassionate man, wanted to run for mayor of his city, because he had some revenge he was dying to serve cold on behalf of Passive and his deceased father-in-law. Passive's father Syrian Boone was head of security for the current mayor of Detroit, who was Mayor Cahill Caesar. Cahill and Syrian were childhood best friends, but once their friendship was tested Cahill buckled. One late working night, Syrian entered Cahill's office to do his regular check, and make sure Cahill was still breathing, and the surroundings weren't breached. When Syrian walked in on Cahill, Cahill was committing infidelity with a King of Diamond's stripper all the top executive men in the D knew as Basil. Syrian practically had a heart attack because Cahill was Syrian's brother-in-law which meant Cahill was cheating on Syrian's sister. Instead of having a heart attack, Syrian snatched Basil off of Cahill's half-naked body and yanked her into the nearest bookshelf, and beat Cahill until he was unrecognizable. Of course Cahill wasn't going to let Syrian get away with beating up the no good mayor so Cahill had Syrian arrested for every charge that the city should've been bringing upon Cahill himself. In rebuttal, Syrian encouraged Cahill to drop all of his pending charges, or he was going to tell his beloved sister about Cahill's faithlessness, and he was going to be the cause of the biggest publicity and scandals surrounding a mayor in history. Cahill thought Syrian was just bluffing, until Syrian started meeting with local news reporters, radio stations, and local magazine editors. Syrian even got a tape recording from Basil with her admitting that she had an affair with the mayor, and she knew three other women who were having an affair with the mayor as well. Once the naked truth began leaking out like water from a leaking pipe, in Cahill's eyes death was the only penalty. A couple days before their trial begun, Cahill had Syrian murdered in prison in his defenseless sleep. At this time, Smoke had just popped the big question to Passive, and Passive couldn't wait to tell her father, and show him her immaculate ring. She always visited him and as much as she could, and her father had shared with her everything he possibly could about Mayor Cahill because he knew his days were numbered. Passive was the main plug to Syrian leaking out all of Mayor Cahill's dirty deeds so she knew everything. The only thing she didn't know was that her father was dead until her last visit went unvisited, and instead of sitting behind a 2-way window gazing into her father's green eyes, she began the grieving process as she found out her father was dead. When those words were murmured to her, she knew exactly who did it and why, and she knew that she wasn't going to die without making sure Mayor Cahill and his affiliates felt her wrath.

Passive's support for her husband was limitless. And she was willing to take all or nothing risks just so that could make everyone responsible for her father's death go straight to hell.

They did practically everything together, and by Smoke becoming a cop, there was a lot of more riskier things they were going to be doing together. During Smoke's first days of being an official cop, there was a lot of talk throughout the precinct about people stealing drugs out of the evidence room. Every single one of those cops got caught, because they weren't smart enough, they weren't fast enough, and they weren't grimy enough, but not Smoke. He had all the qualifications and skills it took to be an inside man. After some soul-searching he decided he was going to steal a load of drugs every full moon, and began a drug enterprise of his own, and his wife was going to be the deliverer. This was a decision that him and Passive made together on behalf of their dreams. They had lots of real estate properties all over the United States, they had lots of connections, they had the perfect motives, they had lots of stamina, and mostly they had each other. As unstoppable as they seemed, the past had a cold reality for them that was more devastating than the future.

Table of Contents

Chapter 1:

Money Is Money

No Matter What Kind Of Money It Is...

"Another Shady Mission, Tricks like Watching Pictures and Hazy Vision

Tonight Is Love Making Take You Any Place You Wish

Today We Satisfy, Yesterday Was Stolen Kisses;"

Keyshia Cole's Playa Cards Right was thumping from Passive's favorite XM radio station.

Interrupting her music flow, Passive's Apple phone was instinctively enabled with talking caller id.

"Call from a restricted number."

Already Passive's mind was racing like two cars on a NASCAR track. *Smoke was supposed to have been back.* Passive kept thinking and re-thinking to herself causing herself to lose all composure.

Being a lady drug transporter definitely had its ups and downs, and the top downfall of their whole drug shipping and handling profession had Passive pacing the hardwood floors in their trap-house like a nervous wreck awaiting her hubby's return. He had to make it back by her side before she could fully self-diagnose herself with paranoia.

Nobody liked to play guessing games with restricted callers. Even with all the geniuses improving cell phone technology, caller ID couldn't even suppress the suspense of a stranger, but in Passive's illegal line of business she was either going to make money or be scared, but she couldn't do both because scared money didn't make no money, and if she missed one call pertaining to a drug contact, her and Smoke would lose-out on a whole forest of dead presidents. Dead presidents that they needed to abundantly touch their hands so they could run their town the way they envisioned it should be ran.

For a quick state of tranquility she thought about the song "Hopeless" by Dionne Ferris off of Love Jones soundtrack before answering the nameless caller who was driven to get an answer since the phone had practically rang a million times.

"Hello," Passive greeted in her small, but seductive pretty little voice. Even if she wanted too she couldn't put any bass in her voice. Often people compared her voice to Marilyn Monroe, but who cares how light or deep her voice is; *money is money*.

"What up P! How you been girl? Is my brother around?" Only one person on the planet ever to Passive's knowledge called her P and that was her husband's backstabbing sister Omani. Hearing Omani's voice immediately made Passive agitated who was already on the verge of sweating bullets. The last thing she needed was somebody like Omani disturbing her peace. Why didn't she let her phone keep ringing, forward her to voice mail, anything, but pick up the damn phone? Why? Why? Why? But I guess that was her small price to pay for not following her first mind.

How did Omani get Passive's number anyway? Then again we are talking about Omani here. A girl who would probably suck and fuck her way to get anything she wanted. A girl whose name you would find in any dictionary up under the word **scandalous**. Omani was nothing more than the typical girl turning tricks for a boss bitch.

"You're the last person that needs to know how I'm doing. And you know I hate when you call me P so 86 that. And if you wanted your brother why didn't you call his phone?" Passive responded salty with more attitude then a smart-mouth, sassy 10-year-old girl back-talking her mother. Clearly, Omani was like dead weight to Passive and to all the other people in her universe she stabbed in the back. Passive didn't call her, Passive didn't see her, nor did Passive ever think about her.

Passive was very careless and narrow-minded when it came to family so establishing a relationship with Omani never would be on her list of things to do. It wasn't like Omani was her immediate family anyway. Not to mention she wasn't about to baby-sit no 18-year-old hypocrite with silly antics, when she was a 23-year-old woman with money, power, and respect.

"I did try calling him, but he

didn't answer," Omani lied. She was just trying to see if Smoke was home before she came over and put a move on Passive. A move that little old Omani conjured up herself, and it didn't help either that Omani had a mindless bitch encouraging her actions. Her mind was more screwed up than a brain tumor because Omani had the truth all fucked up. That's exactly why the truth is not what you think, or what somebody tells you, it's what you know. Always stick to what you know.

▪▪▪▪▪▪▪▪▪▪▪▪▪▪▪▪▪▪▪▪▪▪▪▪▪▪▪▪▪▪

The distance and low profile Omani had to keep was all her fault. The last time Omani and Smoke saw each other was eleven months ago, when Smoke graduated head of his police academy and went straight to a police captain thanks to his connections. Smoke had a huge party at Club Elysium on 625 Shelby Street, celebrating his graduation and quick promotion, and it was him and Passive's 1st married anniversary. The invitation list was exclusive, but that didn't stop people that were uninvited from coming. And the insidious Omani slash Christina Milan look-a- like, blond hair and all arrived on Smoke's red carpet with an unwelcomed and unwanted guest who she knew damn well would cause a bunch of havoc. Guess Omani was trying to make an entrance and a noticeable exit too with Smoke's infamous ex-girlfriend Lindsay. Being bi-sexual and disrespectful, she was certainly sending her family the wrong messages. Her family's enemies should've been hers too, but obviously family wasn't shit when it came to money.

As unbelievable as it appeared Omani and Lindsay weren't secret lovers, they were truly just a team in disguise. If only Smoke and Passive would've saw the picture that was painted before them eleven blurry months ago, that Elysium night of celebration, those two malicious bitches who were arm to arm, ponytail to ponytail, curb to curb. The future problems that lied ahead of them would've been a no brainer even though a lot of time passed by. Enough time to forget what would now be considered as a minor misunderstanding or a call for attention; faces are never forgotten.

Lindsay was like one of those estranged stalkers on a channel 7 soap opera that stayed behind the scenes for ages terrorizing people. Lindsay's excuse for her chaotic behavior was her undivided love for Smoke. She was beyond obsessed. Age 25, skin as rich and creamy as a vanilla wafer, the perfect fashion model height of 5'9', and a stacked 142 pound body that could cover a whole magazine were just her physical assets. Economic stature wise she was snobby rich thanks to her successful, urban magazine her stockbroker daddy helped her establish known as Dirty Raw along with her street affiliations. She was almost ten days away from being Smoke's fiancé before the truth reared its ugly head.

Smoke planned on proposing marriage to Lindsay on her 24th b-day. She was going to get the best ring she never had. Smoke thought he was ready to make that special commitment with the love of his life, which he was, but Lindsay's forces wouldn't allow him to be a fool. All women are crazy or have some type of craziness in them, but Smoke didn't have any idea that Lindsay had certified, stapled, and notarized documented craziness absolutely no idea. Smoke thought Lindsay was so flawless, so perfect, and so truthful.

  Never did Lindsay share her true history with Smoke. The truth began with her record of being a mental institutional patient. She had a picture of herself engraved on the dysfunctional walls of the Rose Hill Center at 5130 Rose Hill Boulevard. Born in a crazy house to her crazy mother Liz Chambers, mental illness was in her blood. Her nanny Corset raised her until Lindsay's mental problems starting setting in, and Corset quit. Lindsay became a tenant at the Rose Hill Center after a spree of "calls for help", until she became 18 and was entitled to her inheritance of 100 million dollars. Lindsay bought her freedom by donating 1 million of those dollars to her mental institution, and agreeing to outpatient care. She stayed low-key, began a stream of street afflictions, and became a business woman. She learned how to conceal her illness from the world, and only trusted herself with this confidential information. She never told anyone about it, and nobody besides her parents would ever know about it. She would honor that until the day she died.

Something was telling Smoke not to marry Lindsay and it wasn't cold feet so he went with his gut feeling and cut her loose. Once the words came out of his mouth that he didn't want to be with her anymore, Lindsay practically killed herself. She jumped through a glass 2-story window like she was trying to escape a fire. When detectives arrived on the scene she tried to lie and say Smoke pushed her out the window until the police saw that she was completely delusional. She kept saying "my husband pushed me, my husband pushed me, even though she was not Smoke's wife, and was never even

Smoke's fiancé. By Smoke being on his way to becoming a cop, and having police connections, it was his word over hers. And his story was, " the bitch tried to kill herself because I dumped her," so his story stuck.

Smoke didn't even bother going to St. John Hospital to visit Lindsay after her suicidal attempt, and after she falsely blamed him of attempted murder trying to bring ashes to his good name. As far as he was concerned the bitch was exed out of his life, and his final words were engraved and set in stone.

Chapter 2:

B Is For Backstabbing

Anyone Is Subject To Be A Backstabber...

How dare Omani make such an ingenious mockery out of all the unforgivable shit that Lindsay represents? Walking arm to arm with her and showcasing her off like a brand new car like nobody in the Mitchell bloodline didn't have beef with her. Even though Omani was obviously the only one cool with Lindsay nobody else was riding on Lindsay's Merry-Go-Round. By the looks of outrage that beamed on familiar faces, eyes were scowling and blood pressures were rising, was confirmation that Lindsay and Omani's plan to turn up Smoke's event was working.

Omani and Lindsay became cooler then cool at a community center kickboxing class. Every bad bitch has a figure to maintain and their strategy just so happened to be utilizing kickboxing techniques. Their instructor Yogi was the best kickboxing instructor in Michigan. Lindsay knew that Omani was Smoke's sister, and her street mouths already informed her how Omani got down so she didn't find her plots to be unachievable at all. Blood is not always thicker than water, and in Omani's case it wasn't.

After Lindsay schemed her way into a mutual friendship with Omani, she made her an offer that her itching hands couldn't refuse. Lindsay never shared any of her motives with Omani; all she did was created a solid case around Passive so Omani would hate Passive as much as Lindsay did. Lindsay planted a lot of seeds in Omani's head, by telling her that she has proof that Passive is a liar, a cheater, and a deceiver, and she just wants the best for Smoke. Omani believed her, when money was talking why wouldn't she believe her when she didn't have anything to lose.

"Omani, I don't know if you know this, but Passive is an international drug dealer."

"You have to be kidding me, I thought Passive was a social worker."

"Your brother doesn't know anything about it. You know drug dealers are beneath him."

"Exactly I know my brother, and I know why he wanted to become a cop. He would never marry a drug dealer."

"I wish I could warn him, but you know as well as I do he has a PPO against me, and even if I could go near that man he wouldn't believe one single word from me."

"Don't worry I will tell him somebody needs too."

"And when you do you should

make it juicy. We got to setup Passive real good. We can't let her get away with this. Straight lying to Smoke all this time making him believe her lies."

"Don't worry I'm going to put a bi-sexual move on her she will never forget."

"What do you mean a bi-sexual move?"

"I'm going to kiss her."

"You just call me when you're on your way over there and I'll make sure everything else falls into place." Lindsay was going to have a field day with this superior kiss.

"I'll toast to that," Omani and Lindsay smacked champagne glasses.

Omani thought she was saving her brother from a backstabbing bitch, but sooner than later she'll find out whom the true backstabbing bitch was.

****

Lucky Smoke's cousin Mellow spotted them two scandalous bitches and brought it to Smoke's attention ASAP.

"I'll be right back baby," Smoke kissed Passive before he slid away with Mellow for some privacy.

"Why is your sister here with Lindsay?"

"You have got to be kidding me?"

"I'm not kidding you at all."

"I don't know what's gotten into Omani, but I don't have time for neither one of them so get rid of them ASAP."

"I got you." Smoke wasn't about to let two unworthy bitches ruin his night so he let the bouncers handle that shit. The super brave, double duo wasn't even in the party for ten minutes before they were picked up by their 16 inch genie ponytails and swung out on the street like two drunken bums. Smoke didn't bother to trouble his wife with this news so he didn't, but he did hold a stern grudge over Omani's appearance with Lindsay for like six months until finally he and Omani squashed it recently, but that was Smoke and Omani. As far as Passive and Omani went- they didn't squash anything.

▪▪▪▪▪▪▪▪▪▪▪▪▪▪▪▪▪▪▪▪▪▪▪▪▪▪▪▪▪▪▪

"I really need to talk to my brother so do you know when he's coming back?"

"What do you of all people have to talk to Smoke about? Really I don't even think I should tell him you called."

"Look I guess you didn't get the memo, but me and Smoke are on speaking terms. I have an important letter- priority mail- I need to give him right away, plus I wanted to know if you needed any workers or work?" *Clearly this bitch has been smoking on rocks or angel dust for her to get off relating me to drug deals. I never told*

31

this girl about my personal business so why is she asking me about workers or work? Somebody been talking to her because I know my name and drugs didn't just fall from the sky and land in her mouth. Smoke must be telling this trick everything about me even though it's not his place to discuss our dirty affiliations with somebody else especially not a backstabbing bitch. But I'm surely bout to get to the bottom of this.

"I don't know what you're talking about Omani, but by all means you can bring the letter."

"Denial is never good Passive, but that's another story for another day. I'm pretty sure you want to get back to doing whatever you was doing just like I want to do the same." Something was up; something was about to hit the fan, Passive knew that soon as they were face to face, a mosquito would even be able to sense the tension that stood between them.

It was only routine for Passive to be close-minded and mean mugging somebody she barely knew and distrusted. But since it's been a while, and she wanted to know exactly what was up Omani's sleeve, and why she wanted to talk to Smoke so bad she decided she would help her out even though she knew better. Money was money, and the only people that have faces when it comes to making money are the dead presidents.

Just let this bitch get cute with me and I swear I'll show her another side of me she never knew existed.

"Where are you? I mean where y'all at however you want me to state it?"

"I'm on the corner of Van Dyke and Emily. The house will be on your right-hand side. If you're coming from 7 mile you'll have to bust a quick left when you see Emily, and if you're coming from 6 mile you'll have to bust a quick right."

"I'm on my way," Omani sneered as she ended her call of deception. Omani called her boss lady as directed and let her know that it was about to go down. Her purple lipstick was about to be smeared all over Passive's sweet little lips. And wasn't shit about to stop her or change her mind from her disloyal intentions.

Disasters loved to strike in the Mitchell family. Whether you married a Mitchell or were born a Mitchell you were still going to be S.O.L (shit out of luck).

Chapter 3:

Red Flags

Never Ignore A Red Flag...

Omani Sade Mitchell was the youngest of a bunch of three. Smoke was the oldest sibling at 29 years of money-making and heart-aching, and the first sibling to be married. As much as Smoke sounds like a street name, it was his middle name, and he was proud of its urban uniqueness. His middle name didn't come out a baby book, and it wasn't a popular neighborhood name either. When Smoke's mother Andrea was in excruciating labor with him at Detroit Receiving Hospital on September 25, 1984 she had all types of smoky hallucinations. The doctors thought that maybe her behavior was caused by the anesthesia, the fear of motherhood, or the displeasure of contractions. Andrea yelled vigorously through the labor floor, "oh my god smoke is coming from the ceiling and were all going to burn, please hurry up and get my son out of me!" Her labor and delivery mirages didn't stop until her 9 pound baby boy was born, and she called him Darnell "Smoke" Mitchell, but Smoke was going to be his official name.

Smoke stood six feet and two inches high; he had a light chocolate tone with a Red Indian glare; every physical aspect about him was picture perfect, and mesmerizing. He had a swagger worth jacking and a wife he wouldn't trade for the world.

The last sibling in line was Kyra, who at 23 looked just like an older version of Omani. The three of them were brought-up by their Aunt Glow who took guardianship of them after their parents disappeared into thin air and left them at Glow's house for a month with no letters, no phone calls, and no-nothing. Their parents claimed to be going on a road trip to get married in Las Vegas, have a short honeymoon and then return so their parents must've never got married because they never returned. It may have taken the kids a long time to catch on, but not Glow. She knew what the deal was the moment her sister Andrea looked in her eyes to even tell her bold face lies.

Truthfully Andrea wanted to be childless, but her mother would've killed Andrea if she got an abortion or given up any one of her babies for adoption. Not only did her mother say "you should've kept your fast legs closed" but her mother said "abortion or adoption over my dead body." And shortly after the birth of Omani, Andrea got her wish when her mother passed away. There was no one or nothing stopping Andrea now from dumping her kids off on someone for good. Mine as well keep them in the family so she chose her sister Glow who was infertile to reap her three biggest mistakes.

To clear things up, Andrea and her children's father Andre planned to get married in Vegas and never come back. Andre was just as heartless as Andrea and that's exactly why they were perfect for each other, but on the way to Vegas Drea and Dre got into a nasty argument because Dre slipped up and told Drea about his other wife so you know Drea went ham. And she had all the reason to go ham, but that didn't stop Dre from head-bunting and dumping her out on the road in the middle of nowhere. He said, "you can get with it or get lost, but this is the way it is." And just like her mother she said "over my dead body." She refused to come second to any bitch and she wasn't about to come second to her children and that is exactly why she neglected them for life.

And just like Smoke, Kyra didn't have much of a relationship with Omani neither after she was highly disrespected and shitted on. Aunt Glow had begged Kyra to take Omani in because her heart was too old to go to war with a young, backstabbing bitch like Omani so Kyra took her in since Aunt Glow was basically like a mother to her. All Kyra asked her sister to do was respect herself, and respect her household, but to Omani those were just small rules meant to be broken. Kyra came home one day and caught Omani recording a threesome with two niggas and a female in Kyra's bedroom that was been supposed to end, but it was just too damn juicy to say cut due to overtime pay. So juicy Omani wanted to join in, but then again she never mixed business with pleasure.

In return Kyra beat the shit out

of Omani and her other female associate which gave enough time for the sexually explicit intruders to scramble their clothes up and get away before Kyra could hit them with that one hitter quitter Smoke taught her growing up and hit them in their sacs. Not only did Kyra kick Omani out of her house, but she kicked Omani out of her life. She disowned Omani as her sister with no regrets. Kyra was so disgusted by Omani's betrayal that she left Michigan and moved to Missouri. She planned to live a happy, honorable life there forever.

Around the time Kyra left Michigan, Omani was losing it because her and her first love Onyx had just broken up, but a couple months later they reunited as roommates when Onyx welcomed her to live with him. What kind of first love would he be to say no when he still wanted access to her, wanted to be able to keep tabs on her, and he heard about her hustler ways. He wanted a piece of the pie too which would be a hand in the rent and food supply. He didn't even care about Omani's street licks long as she kept that shit to a minimum. He mistakenly figured she would calm down a little bit if she had a roof over her head, and lived with the only man she ever loved; the man that had her being so rebellious anyway, but he was wrong.

"I'll be back Onyx I got to make a run," Omani told Onyx who was stretched out on their leather loveseat. She made a speedy exit before the 21 questions began pouring down. Who was he to ask questions of his sort when they weren't together anymore? In his mind, that was still his cutty and as long as they lived together he could ask any got damn question he wanted to.

Onyx got a notion that Omani

was up to something ludicrous as usual by her high speed and her skimpy dress code, but it wasn't his job to be her keeper so he let her be as rotten as she wanted to be. From the second Omani got off the phone with Passive to the second she strapped her seatbelt on, she already had a mental picture of where she was headed so she could arrive to Passive pronto. Time-wise it only took her ten minutes tops on the streets to get to Passive because she knew the streets of Detroit like she knew the lines on the back of her hand. If only she knew somebody was following her whereabouts closely. She was whipping her stick shift Mustang in and out of lanes like she stole something and was on the getaway. Once she got to Passive's location, parked in front of the corner house, and didn't see Smoke's grey Jaguar XK coupe anywhere around the domain that was her q to walk up the first steps of seduction.

Omani got out her car walking just like a temptress and balled up her fist knocking on the front door until she saw Passive standing right across from her knowing that once this visit was over, her boss lady would be very proud. Examining Passive's red stilettos, booty shorts, and white tank top, Omani thought Passive looked more delicious then Beyonce in her Crazy in Love video.

The thing that brought Omani over there so quickly was pure ignobility and her fascination for money. Omani tried not to look all the way in Passive's dark green eyes, but she couldn't help it because it was only natural to look into the deep-end of somebody's eyes when you were speaking to them. Before Passive could read Omani's body language she stepped in the house, closed the front door behind her, and opened her arms up as if she was about to give Passive a big teddy bear hug. Boy did she trick her, because she gave Passive a wet, purple kiss, but not just any kiss, a kiss on the lips. It was a complete kiss too, and Passive froze like Omani gave her a poisonous kiss and every second that their lips touched, more and more venom was being released into Passive's bloodstream. And as they were kissing- they were too far away from the photographer to hear the invisible camera outside of the house clicking.

What the hell was Passive thinking? Passive wasn't thinking. Kissing a girl, kissing somebody else other then Smoke period? Why didn't she use her reflexes like she should've? What happened to the other Passive that was supposed to come out if Omani got cute? Hell she didn't even like Omani. Could she have some bi-curiousness in her?

"You nasty little twit, what the fuck is wrong with you?" Passive yelled at the top of her arteries, wiping off her dirty lips, pushing Omani's back straight into the wall behind them making a picture straddle off of its post and was an inch away from slamming into Omani. Omani should've been one inch closer.

"You know you liked it."

"I should spit on you like trash and drag your ass out of here for that shit." And just as Passive was about to go WWE on Omani Smoke- Passive's husband, Smoke- Omani's brother saved her pathetic little life as he came through the front door.

"Whose Mustang is that outside?" Smoke asked Passive until he noticed Omani who was physically discombobulated because no female besides Kyra had ever laid paws on her like that before.

"Get her out of here now!"

Passive screamed like she was recording a rock n' roll anthem, and stormed into another room.

Whenever Omani came around it meant she was conspiring on somebody that was in a one foot radius of her. And that would be Passive.

Passive had no idea that Omani was bisexual because Smoke never mentioned much to her about Omani and since she wasn't in their immediate circle, she knew it was a reason why. She knew the bitch had to be backstabbing now.

You would think that Smoke wouldn't trust Omani with even half of a candy bar, and he didn't.

"You heard my wife loud and clear so get your shit and get the fuck on!"

"I really need to talk to you Smoke. I don't know what her problem is." Omani tried to change the subject rising up to her feet. At this point she didn't know what Passive was going to do, but she didn't care. Her mission was to kiss her and that's exactly what she did. *Business is business, it's nothing personal. Cheese.*

"If you wanted to talk you should've called me. I don't know what made you think you could just pop up over here without my confirmation and think that everything was going to be peachy."

"I talked to Passive and she gave me directions so I came."

"Passive doesn't know you like I do, and if she did which she will your ass will always be grass."

"But big brother I just wanted too….?"

"Don't give me that big brother shit! I don't know what happened here, and I don't care just leave before I give your ass a big brother ass whopping. And don't you ever bring your ass over here again without my permission."

"Okay I got it I'll leave," Omani said as the door slammed shut and locked behind her, but it didn't matter because all she saw was dollar signs. It didn't register in her head that she just committed the ultimate betrayal. Her young-minded ass didn't know shit about loyalty.

Smoke had to check on Passive and make sure she was okay.

"Do you want to talk about it?"

"No I don't!" Passive hollered at Smoke with intensity. This was the first time in her life that a woman, a woman younger than her at that made a pass at her. And the woman just so happened to be her husband's sister. How do you tell your husband your sister kissed me?

"But I really would've appreciated if you would've told me that your sister liked girls."

"I'm sorry for not telling you that, but just know I have my reasons

48

for keeping certain people out of our lives, and not telling you specific things about those people who aren't welcome in our life. Some things are better left unsaid. Our lives are already too complicated to be distracted by the complexity and negativity of others. Stress, worry, pain, and grief are bad for your heart. And you know that I will never ever hurt you or let anyone hurt you."

"When you put it like that, I totally understand." Even though Passive didn't admit that Omani tried something, Smoke knew Omani tried something. That's just the way she was. She was always trying new things, despite what the consequences were, she never considered consequences. And on top of that Passive had traces of lipstick by her lips wiped off to the edges of her face.

Smoke knew Passive would never let him down, and she would

never let anyone come between them so he wasn't worried about nothing. He wasn't a man of insecurity.

"So everything went smoothly?" Passive tried to snap back into it even though Omani's kiss of death kept replaying in her head.

"You know it- I'm here ain't I?"

After some hugging and holding, Passive and Smoke made sure all the work was straight and checked out the product itself so Passive could hit the road. A lick of the product proved that Passive and Smoke were going to be supplying the dope game this week. Smoke knew exactly what he tasted from teenage experience. He did learn quite a bit about drugs in the police academy, but his lessons in the police academy didn't have shit on his street lessons he gained from his Uncle Sam who was the only father figure Smoke had in his life growing up once his father abandoned him. Instead of teaching Smoke how to be a man Sam taught him how to be a hustler.

Passive's overnight Gucci bag was already packed, and her tank was already gassed up over the F. And as far as mechanically, Passive's Lexus was in top dollar condition. She took care of her cars like she took care of her stilettos; she kept them clean with no scratches and no scuffs always looking fresh off the rack, but there was nothing like a new pair.

Chapter 4:

My Alias Is Diamond

They Call Me Diamond Around

These Parts...

Passive's destination was Louisville, Kentucky which the drive from their spot on Emily was approximately six hours and about ten minutes on the nose. You would think Passive would be a little paranoid driving a little over 350 miles highway time with illegal substances in her trunk, but she had lots of confidence when it came to drug transporting. She completely wiped the fear factor of being caught off her slate. Since Passive had made this trip to Louisville plenty of times, she knew all the hot spots on I-75 and I-65 where the state boys be posted, so she made sure not to drive over or under the speed limit, or fall asleep on the wheel, and since she had an outstanding driving record she knew if she ever got pulled over- the cops would write her a huge ticket before they ever searched her car Not to mention gender wise- a cop would pull over a male from out of town before they pulled over a female out-of-towner.

Passive left Detroit a little after three and reached Kentucky a little after nine o'clock. She was one of them precise, slow-motion drug queens. She never liked to do business on the first day because it took all the fun away so Passive went to her and Smoke's nearest ranch-style vacation home in Louisville.

Hotel and motel stays used to be what was popping, but they weren't secluded enough, and why spend your money on somebody else's shit when you can save money on your own shit? Even though Passive had blow money like that, she spent her blow money wisely. There wasn't no telling when a drought or a recession was going to sneak up on her ass like a bad cold. Not to mention they had an empire they were building.

Once Passive reached their oversized, vacant property due to nighttime, no lights being on, or cars lounging in their half u-shaped driveway, Passive peeked around their southern neighborhood to make sure the coast was clear. After Passive parked she took all the drugs out of her car and hid them in a secret hiding spot in their backyard just like she always did and went in the house to freshen up so she could satiate her hunger.

Smoke and Passive's Louisville house was luxurious and squeaky clean. The front yard and the backyard was nicely trimmed and cut with beautiful green grass, big fluffy bushes, and tall spruce trees thanks to the landscape company they had on payroll. Their backyard was fully loaded with a spacious patio deck, a pond less waterfall, and a sparkling, 7 foot, diamond shaped pool with a Jacuzzi. Point blank their house had lots of perks and special effects that gave it its originality.

Their house had engineered wood floors and Cathedral ceilings with hardly any furniture. Simply because they weren't flashy people, they were barely ever there, and it wasn't their main house. Long as they had the basic living essentials of light, gas, and water that was all that mattered. The kitchen had every appliance and dish it needed, and in their bedroom which was the master bedroom had a movie cinema flat screen TV, a queen size bed, dressers and enough clothes, clothing accessories, and shoes to make a whole Salvation Army.

Seeing that Passive was in the

country now and everything was far away, Passive stopped at the first restaurant slash bar she came too which was the Rumors Restaurant and Raw Bar. On the way in Rumor's this dude had the nerve to bump into her and keep going about his business like he didn't have any manors, but the dude who bumped her knew exactly what he was doing. He was on somebody's payroll too and had plenty of Kodak pictures of his target; enough pictures to have every single body feature of hers programmed in his visual memory forever. He didn't expect to bump into Passive tonight, but he was pleased that he did because he spent every day on the look-out for her especially when he found out she was going to be rolling into town. The oncoming crowd was stopping Passive from turning around and bopping whoever bumped into her. When she finally did get to make a complete spin around she didn't see anybody that resembled the guy that bumped her so rudely, but as big as the world seemed it was small so Passive knew she would bump into old boy again before the end of the night especially since his black and blue Detroit 59/59 and his long ponytail was photographed in her memory.

The restaurant's vibe made Passive feel like she was on an island with all their bright, ocean paintings, and tall, exotic plants. As the night progressed Passive had ate some bomb buffalo wings- the declared best Buffalo wings in Kentucky and French fries, and was drinking back to back shots of Seagram's Extra Smooth Vodka with pineapple juice accommodations of somebody who was really digging her. And as soon as she finished her last shot and sat her shot glass down on the bar, that dude in the 59/59 sat right by her.

"I guess you're the one that's been buying me secret drinks."

"It's not a secret no more," the dude said manly and enticingly.

"Earlier I made a mental note to cuss you out the next time I saw you for bumping into me like you did without apologizing but, I guess these drinks are forgiveness enough."

"I don't know what I would've done if you didn't forgive me and I had to leave here tonight without getting to know you better." Passive looked very precisely at the gentleman's face that was sitting beside her and she noticed a scar, or something that resembled a birthmark.

"What's that on your face if you don't mind me asking?"

"It's my sexy birthmark."

"I never saw a birthmark on nobody's face before."

"I'm pretty sure there are a lot of things you never seen. So what's your name gorgeous?"

"They call me Diamond around these parts," which was a true statement. Every drug dealer or street lord had a street name and Passive's just so happened to be Diamond. Passive had never really seen June up close so it didn't occur to her that she was actually face to face with her connect. Little did Diamond know that the person that was before her, she was nothing, but a target to them, and he had the complete 411 on her, and knew her real name was really Passive Mitchell thanks to Lindsay Chambers.

******

Lindsay and June met at a raunchy Louisville bar, a couple months ago when Lindsay was on a short vacation visiting her sister Marcela who was a Louisville resident also. Marcela was 4 years older than Lindsay, and was her stepsister on behalf of their father's second marriage to Marcela's mother. At first, neither Lindsay nor Marcela knew of each other until Lindsay was released from her psychotic blues at 18, and began making up for lost time.

Marcela and Lindsay were sipping on some happy hour drinks when some stranger kept sending them complementary Margaritas to their table which was June's famous move on how to get a woman. First you buy her a few drinks and then you approach her. Neither Marcela nor Lindsay could figure out which sister the guy wanted, so they just kept laughing and drinking up until finally June felt it was time for the approach. Confidently, he walked his way over to Lindsay's side of the table and sat by her.

"How are you lovely ladies doing? I hope you don't mind if I have a seat." June spoke politely even though she was already sitting down.

"No you good seat yourself."
Both Lindsay and Marcela responded,
but as the conversation progressed
June gave himself away as a man not
into playing games. She told Lindsay
she was digging her, and that she was a
lesbian, and Lindsay's facial
expression along with Marcela's
displayed laughter which was enough
to send June packing, but just when
she was about to knock June's teeth
down her throat for insulting her
sexuality, she kept her fist by her side
as a few bright ideas surfaced through
her rabbit mind. Kindly, she asked
June to remain at their table and
became real chatty with her. After a
few cloudy moments, she knew
exactly how she was going to put her
latest and greatest master plan in
motion. Even though her sister
Marcela was present at the time and
they were supposed to be enjoying
dinner alone, Lindsay carried on.

Marcela knew the way Lindsay felt about Smoke so she didn't trip. She knew it was best to just mind her business because if she said anything about **Smoke** Lindsay would cut her head off. And Marcela knew that as conniving as her sister was trying to be, deceitful people don't go without consequences so she just let June and Lindsay talk amongst her and tried to act like she didn't hear a thing, but the music and the loud talk that was in the background.

The first question Lindsay asked June was, "what's your occupation?"

"I hope I don't get in trouble for telling you this, but I'm a drug dealer and I own my own tattoo parlor down the way."

"Nope you good, everybody has a little hustler in them right, I know I do."

"Why do you ask?" June

questioned Lindsay. "You obviously got something up your sleeve because I know you aren't gay."

"I see your real sharp so let me just break the ice for you. I love this man who has a woman and I want to make their life a living hell so all I want you to do is do the same thing you did to me. Try to get with her every chance you get. "

"First of all is this girl gay?"

"I have proof that she may be that's why you are kind of valuable to me. Money is not an issue so know that I will indeed pay you well. It will certainly be more then what you make as a drug dealer and as a business owner."

"So maybe I should ask what do you do for a living then?"

"Tell you the truth I do a little bit of everything, but mainly I do whatever makes me money."

Before June could ask any

more questions about Passive, Lindsay gave her the whole lowdown. She told her Passive's whole background. She showed June a portfolio full of pictures of Passive like Passive had auditioned for a modeling agency which she did. Only now those modeling pictures were in the hands of Lindsay. The more and more June studied Passive's photos, the more he noticed a familiarity.

"Umm... I know this girl."

"How is that?"

"I deal drugs with her."

"You do huh? That means you have contact with her whenever she comes down here and y'all do y'all thing right?"

"That's right." Lindsay was thrilled to learn something new about Passive and Smoke.

"So next time she comes down here, you already know what to do?"

"I got you."

******

Come to find out the dude that Diamond was flirting with all night long name was June. He was 24, a Scorpio, been a bachelor for a year, was childless, didn't have any brothers or sisters, didn't know much about his family, loved traveling, and was an entrepreneur. And they talked, laughed, and drunk almost to closing time. Still Diamond wasn't drunk, but she was buzzing because she didn't feel the vibrations on her hip as Smoke was calling her unsure if she was safe, still mad at the Omani situation, or something had went wrong. And still June didn't see the big rock Passive had on her ring finger, but he knew she was married and who she was married too, but once he was finished with her, he planned to rip their marriage apart.

"It was nice meeting you June, but I really think it's time for me to be going."

"Can I get your number; you take my number or something?" Flirting was one thing, but Passive never gave her number out. She never cheated on Smoke before besides the kiss with Omani and wasn't going to start cheating on him now just because some little clown at a bar found her attractive and bought her a couple of drinks. What was a couple of drinks when Passive could afford to buy out the whole bar, a bar, or whatever she wanted?

"I'm sure I'll see you around."

"You sure you don't need me to drive you home or wherever you going because I wouldn't mind not to mention I would blame myself if anything happened to you after you left here?" June tried to be courteous.

"No I'm cool; I don't stay far from here."

"But you look like you're about to pass out. I'm not trying to sound like

66

a pest or nothing, but your welcome to spend the night in one of my guest rooms."

'No! Damn!" Diamond showed June her rock.

"Yes I'm married, not engaged, not divorced, and not separated. The conversation was nice, but it's over now so you need to fall back, because I'm about to bounce without you or your number." June was highly disappointed on how Diamond switched up on him, but he wasn't going to give up that easily. He knew he had to keep trying. In his occupation, success, or at least some type of progress was a must. And as for Diamond she could've been left the bar, but she needed a little bit more time sitting down and getting some fresh air, but just to be sure she didn't have to vomit she went to the ladies room where June followed her closely, but undetectably.

After Diamond used the bathroom, she got the shock of her life. It was June standing out in the middle of the bathroom floor with his t-shirt up over his head showing a sports bra, there was some boobs up under that sports bra too, and his pants were down to the floor with his boxers low, low, low as low as they could go, and what appeared to be a strap on was in her grip sneaking between the hole in her boxers. Passive couldn't believe this. Today was like an attack of the twisted women. First it was a bisexual bitch, now it was a stud. Why the hell was she attracting all of these confused ass women? *It was the damn kiss.*

"So you're a fucking a stud? I guess you're just going to take my shit huh?"

"You could just give it to me willingly."

"As slutty as that sounds get the fuck real! I'm not giving up shit willingly or forcefully unless you plan on killing me. I don't think this is a coincidence either me meeting you today." Passive started thinking long and hard. June couldn't understand why Passive was playing hard to get. She knew Passive liked girls and she knew Lindsay didn't show her any Photo shopped pictures.

"I don't know why you fronting I know you like girls."

"Excuse me but I really think you got me twisted up with somebody else! I know you don't know me that well because I'm like a ghost around here. I don't even stay down here!"

"No I don't have you twisted up with anybody Passive." Hearing her real name made Passive freeze, but she tried not to show her true feelings.

"I'm sorry my name is Diamond it's obvious the person you're looking for name is Passive. And that's not me."

"No I know exactly who you are Passive Boone Mitchell. You're married to Smoke Mitchell. You deal drugs for a living and I am in love with your pretty green eyes. I bet you your husband can't do it like this. So what's up because I'm trying to get at you?" This made Passive alarmed even more. How did this girl know her real name, her husband's name, and what she did for a living? *How could she possibly know all of this shit? Nothing was making sense to her right now so she just took it upon herself to leave.* Leave as quickly as she could without making any eye contact with June. And if June tried to grab her she was going to break free no matter what she had to do to break away, but lucky for her June didn't try to stop her.

Still standing half-naked with her dildo hanging in the bathroom, June put her mans up, fixed her clothes and went home, but at the same time she was confused. After her conversations with Lindsay, she was for sure that Passive was going to let her ignite her firebox. In the bathroom, Passive made it appear to June like she was strictly dickly though and didn't have a chance in hell. Maybe because Passive was in Diamond mode, June didn't have a chance in hell or maybe June didn't have a chance in hell to begin with and that's exactly why Lindsay was paying her top dollar. June was trying to figure it out. Passive was trying to figure it out.

Lindsay was too smart for her own good because none of her employees knew about each other so nobody would ever be able to put the pieces to her puzzle together unless a situation arose outside of her control.

Chapter 5:

I Still Love You

My Happily Never After...

It might have seemed a little impossible but, Passive made it home last night and in her bed without falling, crashing, or swerving, but as for today she couldn't stop thinking about all the events that led up to the current hangover she had. Although, the lesbian population was increasing, Passive didn't want to be a statistic. Too her she was still the same Passive/Diamond she has always been. Why all of a suddenly all these perverse females were so attracted to her still had a blank in her mind.

Slowly, Passive moseyed her way to the medicine cabinet and to the kitchen to get a glass of water to take with her two Aleve pills, but she couldn't find a glass, and there weren't any more paper cups.

Damn what is a bitch supposed to drink out of her hand? Passive tore through the kitchen cabinets until finally she came across a box with brand new glasses that wasn't open yet. That just comes to show how rarely Smoke and Passive were in Louisville.

Passive took her two doses gladly and looked at the time on the oven. It was ten in the morning, but usually her contact always called at nine to make sure she was all gravy, but she couldn't recall her phone ringing so she went on a man haunt for her cell phone. Somehow her phone ended up under her bed which made a little sense because her purse was turned over to its side on the floor. Her phone never rang because it was dead. Checking the buttons on her keypad it was obvious Passive needed her charger so she hurried up and plugged it up into the closest outlet. When it finally got some juice- she sprung and turned it on. She figured she'll finally call Smoke before he drove down there and found out what was really going on for himself.

"Smoke I'm okay please don't be upset with me; I'm really not feeling like myself." Passive spoke abruptly before Smoke could go hard on her, but that didn't work so well.

"I don't care what the situation is or how you feeling. All you had to do was call, all the shit I risk for you? What the fuck do you have a cell phone for if you're not going to use it? All I wanted to know was if you were okay. Anything could've happened to you. I was one hour away from calling off of work and tearing the city of Louisville apart to find you. Is that what you wanted?" Passive was just cruising through the house mocking him and making blah, blah faces and as she was doing that her contact was clicking in on the other line so Passive just clicked over without interrupting Smoke figuring he would still be talking by the time she clicked back over.

"Hello."

"Yeah is everything peachy?" A familiar voice gave Passive chills, but she still proceeded with the plans.

"Yep same time, same place. You get yours after I get mines." The directions that Passive worked with were very discreet, but that was just the way you had to do things in a dirty industry like the drug game. If you didn't perfect your own way of doing things and you didn't stick to it- the chances of survival in the game was going to be slim to none. So basically Passive dropped off the drugs in a garbage can in an alley, and twenty minutes later after the contact checked the drugs out he left her the cash in another garbage can they considered mark 2, and then he called her and gave her the go to get her cash. She hoped everything was going to go as smoothly as it always went even though she felt like something or somebody was questionable.

Passive clicked back over though and as she figured Smoke was still talking up a storm. "Okay baby I'm sorry for being so inconsiderate and not calling you, but can I go now?"

"Whatever we'll finish this later."

Really Passive didn't have to go she just wanted to hurry up and get off the phone with Smoke even though it was her fault he was talking to her like he was on his male period. Since Passive's head was still pounding she threw herself back up under the covers to catch an afternoon dream.

*****

Back at home things weren't going so good for Omani, but it was foolish of her to ever think she could have a happy home with her ex-boyfriend. Although, her pockets were full of dirty money thanks to Lindsay Chambers; her love life or should we say house life with her ex was shitty.

Onyx stayed out all night a lot of times which was completely fine with Omani, but he never brought another bitch home especially not in her presence. It wasn't like she had strict rules against Onyx having female company, but it was respect that Onyx was lacking, and respect is something that comes naturally. You can't tell anybody how to respect you, either they do or they don't. Either they will or they won't. But Omani didn't know squat about respect in the first place, and even if she did, you get respect when you deserve it. And if you take all of Omani's street decisions into consideration, she didn't deserve any damn respect from even a fly in the sky.

Omani was just kicking back watching TV in the living room when they came in looking all washed up and dried out. Onyx still had on his clothes from yesterday, and the chick he was looked like she was a part of the itty bitty titty committee, and like her ass was made up of booty shots. She should've stayed at home longer to flat iron her wild mermaid weave, only had on one eyelash, and was missing a bra. Omani hoped that if Onyx hand-picked this chick himself- he didn't do it in the dark because it was clear in the light she had more flaws then Shrek; but ex-girlfriends were the harshest critics.

"Omani this is my friend Tia, and Tia this is my roommate Omani," Immediately Omani got irritated which is exactly what Onyx wanted her to do. The only reason he brought Tia to the house was to make her jealous and to see if she still cared about him the way he still cared about her. Tia wasn't his type of chick period. She was just good for a one-night stand, and that was it. Showing signs of maturity, Onyx was growing tired of fucking random bitches and wanted to concentrate on establishing something long-term; something like what him and Omani use to have, somebody he could be vulnerable with, something irreplaceable.

"EX-girlfriend slash roommate." Omani added determined to get the last word. Either Onyx really wanted to see a chic fight, or he really underestimated Omani and her true feelings.

"I don't know why you felt the need to let that be known, but I guess." Tia commented.

"Would you like something to drink?" Onyx asked Tia.

"Oh no you don't, this bitch

don't buy no groceries here, and I don't support her, if she wants something to drink you better take her ass to the store and buy her something."

"Come on now Omani don't be like that."

"Right Omani y'all aren't together no more, don't be like that," Tia and Onyx kissed. They stayed cooped up in the kitchen for a long while, and Omani stayed where she lay, watching her favorite DMX movie which was Belly.

"I could've sworn when people have company their roommates are supposed to give them privacy." Tia blurted out the corners of her cutting eyes.

"My bad Tia would you like me to go to my room, close my door, and don't come out until you leave?"

"Yeah you get the idea."
Omani rose to her feet exposing her 2-piece lingerie set. Onyx was blown

away by his ex's body. He was beginning to wonder why he let all that go.

"Well no I don't get it. This is half of my motherfucking house to and I'm not about to leave this room or any room in this place for no hoe. And I don't want your cheap ass perfume on my furniture so stay over there!" All Tia could do was stare at what Omani had on and wonder what was really going on here.

"You let this bitch walk around like this?"

"Why the fuck are you so surprised? This nigga isn't my fucking daddy. He doesn't have any say in what I wear or when I wear it. You lucky I wasn't sitting up in here naked. What kind of man complains about seeing a woman in some lingerie? Just listen. Do you hear him complaining now? It's not shit he haven't never seen before."

"Why aren't you saying anything to her Onyx you're just going to let her talk to me like this?"

"You got a mouth if you don't like the way I'm talking to you do something about it?" Tia glanced at Onyx then she glanced at Omani long and hard.

"You know what call me when you get finished bitching up to your roommate," Tia left like she was going to be missed. And probably even thought that Onyx was going to chase after her ass, but he didn't.

"Why'd you do that Omani?"

"I didn't do anything, but speak my mind. We might be roommates, but that still don't give you a right to be bringing bitches up in here all up in my face. Plus you should be glad I said something to that bitch because she was scary. She didn't even want to stand up to little old me. I'm a little bitch and I didn't even touch the girl-

82

she still left."

"But Omani it doesn't matter we aren't together and were both grown, but what you did, how you just handled yourself that was immature. Maybe we need to reconsider this living arrangement."

"We don't need to reconsider shit. I pay to be here just like you do."

"Well just because you haven't moved on yet doesn't mean I haven't."

"Negro please I'm not trying to hold you back from no bitch just don't bring the bitch up in here! You know I don't trust bitches like that. And we work hard for everything we got up in here. I don't know the bitch that well and neither do you so if you want to fuck the bitch you better get a room. Shit you got money and if you don't you better find a bitch that do agreed?" Funny Omani said she doesn't trust bitches like that, that was a lie because she trusted Lindsay easy as hell.

"I guess agreed. And by the way you're killing it in that lingerie." While Onyx was trying to act like there were so many better opportunities out there better then Omani, he knew deep down inside he was still crazy in love with her.

"I saw you looking." And to be honest Omani still had strong feelings for Onyx and she didn't want to see him with any other woman other then herself even though she only seemed to be interested in women. The only reason she ever became bi-sexual was because Onyx was the only man she had ever been with and wanted to be with, and since she couldn't be with him she turned to women. Women were her poison ivy, and men didn't have a chance in hell.

Chapter 6:

Give Me More

Won't Stop, Can't Stop

At the 11th precinct, Smoke spent the whole day wallowing in a meeting with other fellow police officers about alleged stolen drugs. Knowing that his scam was only getting more and more risky didn't raise a drop of sweat to come raining out of his pores, or him to rethink profiting from the drug community. Instead he was thinking of ways to keep his secret enterprise going the whole time.

Smoke went from cop to dirty cop within two months of his arrival to the police department. So far he and Passive had made billions of dollars off of the evidence room, and had only been bartering drugs for six months. Their city dreams had their nose wide open. Once you get your hands on dirty money, it's like a curse, because you can't just shake it off. Motivation was on every corner, every black alley, and every hustler's crevices. Tired of seeing their city fall apart, they made what was a power move in their eyes. Smoke came in to the evidence room and bagged up a product whenever he got lead of a new shipment of the evidence room restocking.

The police chiefs and commanders still didn't have a clue about who the thief or thieves was, or how many times the thief stole alleged drugs, or the amount the stolen drugs totaled too, they just knew they had a dirty cop on their hands. They should've installed some damn video cameras then versus relying on some dumb ass sign-in sheets that at any point of time could go unsigned like all of Smoke's stolen attempts.

Sleep or awake, Billy would always let Smoke slide into the

evidence room without signing the sign-in sheet and he would always let Smoke persuade him into leaving his post for a break so Billy couldn't vouch anything. Truthfully, he was old as dirt and wanted to retire anyway, and now he was getting his wish. To show they meant business they felt the only sensible thing to do was fire sleeping beauty Billy and hire somebody else who could work the evidence room with six eyes which meant Smoke was obviously going to have to make a pat with whoever the new evidence clerk was if he wanted to keep making millions with Passive. Towards the end of the meeting, after all the serious jail time, job losses, and bad reputation for life speeches came the new sexy office clerk who was obviously a new young female to the department, but her presence wasn't a coincidence. Some strings got pulled for her, and the price was right. Along with Omani and June, she was one of Lindsay's little puppets. Her name was Shania, and she was a beige mixture of Puerto Rican and Black. She was the first female to work at the 11th precinct in two years. It used to be an equal number of female and male officers until an abundance of females sued the 11th precinct for sexual harassment.

All the officers were on Shania's tip, and Smoke was looking too, he just didn't make his like so obvious. Little did Smoke know that Shania was already on to him and he was the first man and only man that she was really peeping out when she strolled into the meeting. Not to mention Shania had more motives on Smoke then the criminals that the police dealt with on a daily basis did committing crimes. No matter what position Smoke had in the bachelor game he was on her get list period, and she was willing to get him at all costs. How one look could have a person coo-coo for Coca Puffs so soon wasn't a no-brainer, but it meant that somehow Smoke and Passive both attracted the same kind of people which would explain their compatibility.

Once the meeting was over and so was The Shania Show, Smoke figured he would tell Passive about their unfortunate dilemma, and the business proposal that was ahead of them which just might lead to the end of their marriage.

"What up bay," Passive answered Smoke's call in a sleepy voice that was still in Kentucky.

"Were you sleeping?"

"Yeah but it's time for me to get up anyway."

"Do you want to hear the bad news or the good news first?"

"Tell me the bad news first of

course."

"Well they fired Billy and replaced him with this young chick named Shania. And the good news is they have no idea who the thief is or how many actual times we've stolen shit." This information was certainly gritty enough to make Passive sit upright, and wake her completely up without even the slightest feeling of tiresome. Not only did she have to be worried about two females who were profoundly appealing to her gravitational pull, but now she had to be distressed by a woman tempting her husband.

"Well what do you want to do about this new bitch?"

"The only way to keep the hustle is to get close to her."

"You mean like boyfriend/girlfriend close?" Passive tried to read between Smoke's lines.

"Yeah I do unfortunately."

"Yeah you do that shit, but don't get lost in her because if you do I'm gone." Passive knew off rip that Smoke remaining faithful to her was about to be like man walking on water. It wasn't going to happen. She knew shit was about to get real deep, but how deep and under what conflicts was going to be the question. But who was she to complain or act like she was a saint when she let her husband's sister kiss her and didn't do anything about it?

"I hope things don't go that far."

"Well things aren't about to be a walk in the park. It's never easy to play with somebody's heart, let alone play with yours and theirs."

"I'm not making this decision by myself. If you are so against what the future can bring, the only thing you can do is change the present. Here's your chance to tell me if you're in it to win it or if you want to quit. You have your part and I have mines. I don't know why you tripping were in this together though."

"Yeah but I can see what you can't obviously. And since I'm speechless right now I'll just see you when I get home."

"Alright then I love you." Smoke could feel Passive slipping away already, but how could she be mad, she was only in it for the money even though she was doing the selling- Smoke losses were way more than Passive's hands down. Not to mention she kissed a girl who wasn't just a random girl and was her husband's sister. And yet she was worried about being cheated on like she was Miss Innocent.

*****

It was three more hours before she had to make the drop. She certainly wasn't just about to spend

180 minutes in the house looking at the walls so she put her sexy on and decided she would get a tattoo. Driving down the road, Passive finally found a tattoo shop fifteen minutes later with a blinking blue neon sign that said Black Ink Tattoos. Before Passive got out the car she thought about what tattoo she wanted and the first thing that came to her mind was a tiger so she went in with at least what she wanted, but she forgot to consider colors, size, or the place on her body she wanted her tattoo at.

"Can I help you?" a white receptionist name Becky asked with corn rows who looked just like the white girl-Taryn Manning on Hustle and Flow.

"Yeah I wanted to get a tattoo."

"Can I see your ID?"

"Are you serious they don't even card me at the casino, the club, or the liquor store?"

"You should take it as a complement."

"Well I take it as an insult. Don't you see this big old rock on my finger? That should tell you something about my age."

"Yeah, but your ID will tell me everything." Lucky for Black Ink Tattoos they didn't lose a customer because Passive didn't have time to stop or look for another tattoo shop so she just scrambled for her ID and made the white girl feel real stupid when Becky saw that Passive was from Michigan, and that she was of age.

"Oh so what brings you down here?"

"You mighty nosey aren't you?"

"Okay well you can take a look at our tattoo books to look at our work, and our artist Trace is going to be free next so I'll put you down for him." Passive took a seat and in no time

94

Trace called her name after he reviewed the sign-in sheet. Dressed in a white beater and some plaid shorts, his muscle game was Powerhouse Gym crazy. Trace took Passive to his little spot and it was the last room in the shop.

"2-7-0 what tattoo can I do for you boo? Hold on let me guess I bet you one of them girls that like them hidden tattoos on your chest or ass cheek? Passive had already sat down in Trace's chair. She thought highly of him until he opened up his mouth and she saw his platinum grill. She hoped and prayed her tattoo was going to look like a piece of Mozart art for all this country gibberish she was about to listen too.

"Look I got shit to do so you can save all that extra shit and just tat me up, I want a big ass tiger at the tip of my spine and I want it to look like its crawling up my back and scratching me." Passive showed Trace a page in one of their tattoo books for an example.

"And I don't want any color. I just want it outlined and detailed in black."

"Okay cool take your shirt off for me. I'll have you out in an hour or less." Once Trace got started- Passive wasn't even moved by the piercing needle in her back even though it was her first tattoo and spinal tattoos hurt the worst. She obviously had a high tolerance for pain. Trace was done just as quickly as he said he was going to be. Before he bandaged her up and gave her A&D instructions he took a picture of Passive's tattoo on his digital camera and showed it to her. Trace couldn't talk worth a lick, but he was a cold ass tattoo artist.

"Good looking out I love it."

"I'm glad you do. You don't have to worry about the whole 10 day rule because we only use water proof ink here." Black Ink Tattoos started off at fifty dollars, and they went up fifty dollars by the hour, but Passive just threw Trace four hundred crisp dollar bills, and as soon as she walked out of Trace's room she saw that familiar face again at the counter talking to Becky.

"What did you get Passive?" Becky asked.

"I'm sorry, no I'm not sorry, but I got to go."

"So your name is Passive. I thought your name was Diamond." June spoke, but Passive was already out the door in the parking lot. *Damn what is this bitch psychic? I'm so glad I'm about to go back home. I can't wait to make the drop so I can burn rubber out of here.*

"Becky I got to make a run BRB." June left.

"Alright boss." Unfortunately Passive was still sitting in the parking lot like she had to warm up her car. She should've been thinking on the go, but she wasn't. June spotted her in her jet black Lexus. And when Passive took off so did June. Passive drove back to her house to get the drugs. Of course June was too far back to see exactly what Passive was doing, but she knew she was loading up something **exclusive** in her trunk. And she didn't need eyes to see that Passive was retrieving their drugs. The drop off time was right around the corner so Passive made her way to the drop-off spot still with June trailing her like an undercover cop.

Connects were supposed to be **exclusive**, but there was nothing exclusive about Diamond anymore. Her cover was discovered and the best thing for Smoke and Passive to do was to find another connect because once a connect knew where you lived, knew where your stash was at, even knew more than your name, they couldn't be trusted.

Passive hurried up and scurried away from secret location #1. And when June felt the coast was clear she collected the drugs. Diamond never bullshitted her so she did a half ass check and made her way to station #2 so she could drop Diamond's money off. After the money was completely inside the can June called Diamond.

"Everything is peachy." June spoke in code.

"See you wouldn't want to be you." Diamond ended. June was still sitting off to the side watching Diamond when she came to claim her money wanting to get a long look at her before she disappeared back to wherever she was going. And once Diamond took off so did June who wanted closer relations with Passive. She wished she could have a woman of her stature, but it wasn't enough wishful thinking for that want.

Chapter 7:

We Need A Resolution

Something's Got To Give...

Never did the queasiness and uneasiness of being homesick ever come over Passive until she met June. She loved traveling to Kentucky by herself, and would usually have to force herself to come back home after she made her cocaine money or whatever drug she had to distribute to her buyers, but this time she was in a rush to get the hell out of Kentucky before June saw her again and gave her the creeps.

Passive rode home silently, without one tune, one station, or one beat. She just speculated heavily about how she was going to resolve the whole June situation, but with a mastermind trying to ruin your life there wasn't enough thinking in the world. She wanted to tell Smoke about this June character, but she kind of wanted to get an outside opinion, but how would she get an outside opinion being friendless? How could she get an outside opinion when the only person she chose to communicate with was her husband because she knew how quickly family and friends could become backstabbers?

Lost in her own space on her trip home, Passive stopped to stare into the blue waves of the Ohio River once she rode through Downtown Ohio. She found a little passageway where she could park her car and get a deep glimpse into the river of thought as the sun headed for the west. There wasn't anybody surrounding Passive and her sudden peace, but the breeze and the trees. As Passive sat on a large rock near the water, wedding bells were ringing in her head and her sudden thoughts relived her wedding vows. *I vowed never to make any secrets that I would have to keep and drive me crazy every day. I vowed to be faithful until the end of time. And I wasn't. How am I supposed to tell my partner in crime I kissed his baby sister on the lips without causing him pain? And how am I supposed to handle my first stalker without killing them?*

Passive was so attractive she could never stay anywhere alone for too long without someone joining her.

"If you think any harder, you're going to find yourself with a headache." A real man approached her with an Adams Apple and all. Passive had to be sure this time since the people that she had been meeting lately seemed to have a battle of the sexes.

"Is it that obvious how hard I'm thinking?" Passive asked the strange man dressed in bay white. The kind of white you wear to the beach at this time of day and watch the wind blow through.

"Yeah it is, but I know you were thinking because I come here to think all the time."

"I know I don't know you, but opinions don't have any faces so if you don't mind do you think you can spare your opinion for me?"

"I can do that for you," the man grabbed a seat on a rock close to Passive.

"What would you do if you had somebody stalking you to a threatening point?"

"I would kill them."

"See that's the thing I've never killed anybody before so you can understand why the thought of me killing is hard to digest."

"It is, but a woman's got to do what a woman's got to do even if she has to do the unthinkable." Passive thought on what she just heard for a couple of minutes. And when she turned her head to look at the good advice giver who sat beside her- there was no one there. It was just her again along with the breeze, and the trees.

****

Meanwhile it was almost 12 o'clock at night in Detroit and Shania was still awake going through emotional battles with herself. She lived in a cozy condo in St. Clair Shores by herself and had been single for almost a year. Shania's last relationship ended around the time she graduated from Macomb County Community College with her associate's degree to become a secretary. She had been struggling to find a job until she met Lindsay at a job fair at Cobo Hall who claimed to be a job recruiter for her magazine (Dirty Raw) and have all the connections that Shania needed to get her on, but it was a catch. It was always a catch. Lindsay wasn't trying to hire anybody to work for her magazine really- she wanted people that were interested in her hood, dirty affiliations. And the catch was that Shania was going to have to become a part of Lindsay's greasy plan to break-up Passive and Smoke and she was so desperate she agreed.

Shania's issues wouldn't let her have a good night's sleep so she took her issues into the hallway and start banging her head against the hallway walls as beautiful as she was even though her future was going to be black and ugly. What was possibly going on in her life now to make her indulge in self-abuse? She bit her luscious lips hard enough to leave sores on them that looked worst then a cold sore. Then she punched herself in her left eye until even the true color of her eyes resembled black. And then she began rubbing her back against the sharp edges of her glass tables until small cuts were striped across her back looking like a trail of lines in a plaid shirt until her back was numb and her legs became so weak she fell to the floor, and actually fell asleep to the numbness of her bruises on the floor, but it was all a game. Shania was just beating herself alive as a publicity stunt to get one man's attention; to get one man's affection. And either Shania was going to wear pounds of make-up to cover-up her damages, put on a hat, swoop her hair down over her scars, or let the men at her job have a field day wondering if she was the devil or if she was sleeping with the devil. Even better Smoke, the only man who Shania would date at the precinct would console her. She would just have to wait to work and see.

****

When Passive finally made it home she was sure Smoke was going to be drugged up sleep like people sleep in the hospital after surgery when nothing or no one would be able to wake him up except his alarm clock when and if he heard it going off, but he wasn't. Passive found him sitting on their living room sofa gazing into the dark.

"Why aren't you sleeping baby?"

"I couldn't go to sleep." Passive sat right on Smoke's lap after she locked the door back, sat her bags down, and cuddled up real close to him.

"Well since your woke I have something to tell you and something to show you."

"Tell me what you got to tell me first because I might not want to see what you got to show me after you tell me whatever it is you got to tell me." Passive had to take a couple of deep breathes before she made her one confession even though she really had more confessing to do.

"While I was in Kentucky I met this really forward stud named June and everywhere I went she was there like she had a GPS tracking system hooked onto me or something. Not to mention she reminds me of somebody that we know I just can't put my finger on it yet. I went out to a restaurant where I met her at and I found out he was really a she when she tried to fuck me in the ladies bathroom. And she knows my government name is Passive Boone Mitchell, that I'm married and, that your name is Smoke Mitchell. I don't know what we should do about her, but I swear if I see her one more time, I'm going to do something I'm going to regret." *Stud* and the name *June* stood out to Smoke since the female contact they did most of their business with name was June, and she was a stud. Not to mention Smoke knew mainly all of the drug lords in

Kentucky and none of them were a stud or went by the name of June so they had to be talking about the same person.

Smoke tried to keep his composure throughout the whole time Passive was confirming these things to him about June, but it was mighty hard because the person he was breaking bread with was disloyal and had life all jacked up if she thought her actions were going to go untouched.

"I just got one question and that's does the June you met have a birthmark, that looks like a scar on the side of his face?" Passive pictured June's face in her mind, before she answered her husband.

"Yes she did."

"Don't worry about that I got something for this June character." Smoke assured his wife.

"Oh you're just going to take care of it just like that huh?"

"You know you my Bonnie and I'm your Clyde."

"Well do that shit then," This time Passive gave Smoke playful kisses and Smoke carried her into their bedroom after she showed him her tattoo which was definitely going to spoil some of their love-making because there would be no front-ward body banging. Passive knew she got carried away with the "I want to do it lift" so she figured she would go ahead and give her man a hit of her sweet nectar until her sweet nectar put Smoke to sleep.

For the most part Smoke was a morning person so the sleep he missed on the behalf of his wife's body didn't leave him weary. He actually felt more energetic than ever. Smoke made him a homemade breakfast sandwich, showered, threw on his uniform and belt with gadgets, and sprayed himself with a click of Bora Bora because he liked to go to work smelling good. Little did he know the flamboyant smell of his man cologne would go unnoticed to Shania's unknown cause of brutality.

Shania didn't even bother to come into work late, throw on no stunner shades, or extra make-up. She actually came into work early. She didn't wear her long thick hair down neither to cover up her self-inflicted mutilation, the ones that her clothes didn't cover up that is. She was just as lively, humming songs, and in happy land like she was perfectly fine despite the traces of abuse she had, but how could she be mad when she did this proposed abuse to herself unless she wanted to make the after affect of abuse more realistic. Shania had some nerve though making a mockery out of abuse like abuse wasn't a global epidemic like abuse is funny. Of course everybody wanted to know-what happened to her?

Her answer was "....me and my boyfriend got into a fight, but don't worry I beat his ass too," Shania told a group of inquiring men not including Smoke.

"You're not going to file no report or nothing?" One officer asked.

"Just because I'm employed at a police station doesn't mean I want to control my love life by calling onto the police every time something happens to me. Shit I'm not a victim; I might have some minor scrapes and contusions, but victims are sad. Do I look sad to you?" Shania flashed the biggest, fakest smile ever.

"No." The group replied.

"Well scat than stop acting like y'all haven't never seen somebody get hit in they face a couple of times." It was crazy how Shania had everybody worked up believing her lying ass and feeling her pain. It was two police officers mainly that her story really touched. Their names were Officer Black and Officer Rodgers who were just as young as her and they planned to go pay her little boyfriend a visit and beat his ass for putting his hands on a woman, a friend, and a beautiful woman at that whenever things died down a little bit surrounding the whole abuse ordeal.

By lunch time Shania had all kinds of flowers, sympathy cards, and teddy bears in her work area, but still she was wondering why she hasn't saw Smoke yet. She was almost about to have a bitch-fit and go haywire if she didn't see the man she wanted to ignite her fire, and then there he was stumbling right before her. Smoke thought he would just flirt with her with his eyes, but that got ruined by Shania's beat-up face. His eyes got real big like if they got any bigger they were going to pop out of his eye sockets so he bent down and faked tying his shoes to get his composure back together. When Smoke's shock was under control, the thought growing through his head seized, and the muscles in his face were done making crazy faces he approached her.

"I was wondering when you were going to pop up over here." Shania spoke first.

"Why were you looking for me?"

"No I just see everybody else like fifty times a day except you and I like that."

"That's because I'm not like none of these lame cats around here hounding you like hungry dogs."

"I get that vibe from you."

"I don't know what's going on in your life, but you look like you could use a nice lunch at a nice restaurant."

"I could so when you talking?"

"I got to train somebody today so we'll see what's on the agenda for tomorrow which Smoke was kind of hoeing Shania because tomorrow was Saturday and they didn't work on Saturdays, but she was so happy just to be face to face with Smoke she just agreed.

"Alright I'm ready whenever you are." When Smoke was out of Shania's sight she blushed hard as hell, and made a lot of winning gestures like she was on top of her game and just knew she was going to be wifey status in no time or so she thought even though Smoke didn't ask not one question about her dented face, and she didn't know any facts about Smoke besides what the devil Lindsay told her.

Seeing the blackness on Shania's face showed that Shania had a significant other and made Smoke hate having to become close to her even more because now Smoke and Passive were going to have to deal with all of Shania's problems including her relationship. Damn it already seemed like a lot of shit just looking in and Smoke didn't even know all of the facts yet. Was it really all worth it? Hell yeah drama was a motherfucker, but it made life so much more interesting. Not to mention sex was going to be down the road he was going whether he wanted to believe it now or not. People thought the things you do for love was crazy, but in Smoke's world crazy was the things he was doing for love and money.

Chapter 8:

Anonymous

What you don't know will hurt you...

Passive never liked staying in the house all day on her off days or any days. She had to be on the move, passing time somehow, or spending money so she took a couple of stacks out of her cookie jar stash and went to her car to bring in the duffel bags stuffed with money, but she saw her car was empty which meant Smoke had brought the bags in before he went to work.

When Passive was showering she remembered she had a dream last night. At first she couldn't recall who was in it, or what her dream was about until she kept forcing her brain to think and it hit her when Omani's name kept being tossed around her head like a coin toss. Passive was positive now her backstabbing sister in law had a thing for her, but how was she going to make Omani fall back.

In the dream Omani didn't have one piece of clothing on her flawless body and neither did Passive. They were just plain naked except for the jewelry that dangled from the remaining parts of their body since the two of them stayed icy at all times. Passive never thought she would enjoy seeing a woman naked so much before, but she did. She was captivated by every inch of Omani's frame, and wanted to squeeze and massage Omani's perky breasts while Omani lady-long stroked her, but before Passive's hands could grip Omani's breasts, Omani penetrated Passive's pussy with her dick. It was a strap-on, but she worked it like it was the real thing. Omani laid her body up against Passive's body determined to touch her smooth skin while she licked and kissed Passive on her neck and had her coming, moaning, and squirming like crazy in her and Smoke's bed. And just when Passive was about to splash her waterfalls on Omani yet again she woke-up.

Passive was now showering thinking about what it would be like, and what it would feel like to do it to a girl. She already kissed a girl so she could scratch that off her list of things she never done before. Either Omani's kiss had her gone, she didn't hate June as much as she thought, and really wanted June to put it on her that night in Kentucky, or she was really becoming confused about her sexuality. Girls seemed to be loving her more than boys did anyway so why not. Same sex cheating was certainly not going to be as bad as Passive cheating on Smoke with another man not to say any type of cheating was okay. They say a dream is a terrible thing to waste and in this case Passive kind of wanted to make her dream come true. She felt obligated to throw the whole Omani fall back ideas on the back burner because even in the shower Passive's twat was wet, and she couldn't wait for it to get wetter, but really she just wanted to be prepared for Smoke's unfaithfulness if he went off on the deep-end with Shania. There wasn't any shame in thinking anyway.

Soon as she got completely dressed she thought she was going to zoom right off the block, but she was sadly mistaken. Her problems began with the Mexican mailman who was exiting out of the front yard.

The Mexican mailman named Larry made it his job to always personally hand Passive her mail. He put everybody else's mail in their mailboxes as accordingly, but not Passive's. Larry handed Passive some bills, and a long, brown envelope that was addressed incorrectly. It was mailed to the right address, it had a stamp on it, but whoever sent it left their address section blank, and the name that it was addressed to read **"Diamond Mitchell."** Now this was very fishy.

"Is this a case of the wrong address?" Larry asked who of course had to separate the mail.

"No it's not I got a sister named Diamond." Passive lied trying to conceal the mysteriousness she felt about who was sending her mail to her alias name. Passive wondered if she should tell Smoke first before she opened the envelope, but who knew what the contents included. The only way to find out was to open it up.

"Thanks Larry, but I got to go." Passive ran in the house and almost bust her ass trying to open up her brown package. When Passive reached inside of the brown boundaries, she found three unbelievable things. First, it was a bunch of black and white 8" by 10" pictures of her and Omani kissing. That was the last thing Passive wanted to see; the day she locked lips with her husband's sister. Second, it was a little note wrote in cursive writing that slipped out too.

Dear Diamond,

I bet you thought you had a secret, but you didn't. Secrets never go un-kept especially not this one. I can't wait until Smoke finds out what you did, and leaves your ass because that is exactly what he's going to do. And you know it, that's probably exactly why your face is probably all torn up right now. I should send a photographer to take a picture of your facial expression right now too because that's a Kodak moment. I know you don't have a clue who I am, but let's just say you do know me very

well, and when everything comes out
to light including your disloyalty I will
be right there by Smoke's side and
everything will not be a blur then, and
that big ass rock you got on your
finger will be mine.

See you in a
minute bitch!!!!!

And the third piece of content
was a magazine that was going to be
the September issue of Dirty Raw. It
had Passive and Omani kissing all over
the cover of it. That magazine was
going to be hitting shelves soon.
Passive had no idea that Lindsay
Chambers had a magazine or this was
Lindsay Chamber's magazine. Short
stories were the only pieces of
information that Passive had on
Lindsay, and each one of those stories
came from Smoke's mouth. Passive
had never ever even laid eyes on her

worst enemy, or seen some throwback pictures of her. Lindsay was just that unreal to Smoke and his memory.

Talk about a rude awakening. The letter that Passive just received changes everything because now her ass was on the chopping block and there was no way to get around the chopping block she was on, but to confess her sins to Smoke and hope that he forgave her. She had to do something before this anonymous person got to him first. Passive didn't know who in the hell was doing this to her, but now she was really starting to hate her life and the mistake she made kissing Omani. I hate you was just a couple small words to Passive now, because everything that she was going through was mostly Omani's fault and she hated her with a passion. Passive knew Omani had something up her sleeve the moment she came around and this was the big bang. She should've kept her distance from Omani just like she opted too, but before Passive really had it out for Omani she decided to call her and ask her what the hell was these pictures and this magazine about.

Omani's phone rang for a long time until her voicemail finally picked up, but Passive wasn't finish. She continued to keep calling back until finally Omani answered.

"So this is the real Omani, the Omani that likes setting up people?"

"What are you talking about Passive?"

"Why the fuck do I have photographs coming to my house of us kissing, and why are we on the cover of a magazine?

"Well since you want to ask questions why the fuck have you been lying to my brother all this time telling him you are a social worker. When you and I both know you're not a damn social worker?"

"So what am I Omani?"

"You are an international drug queen. You go by the alias Diamond. You are a lying bitch who my brother would've never married if he knew your truths? Passive wanted answers and the only way she knew she would be able to get them is to keep this conversation going. She didn't know how in the hell Omani knew all this shit, but she had to find out.

"All that is true Omani, I run missions for your brother. We are in this game together. He knows everything."

"'You have to be kidding me?"

"I'm not kidding you Omani, but apparently you let somebody else make a fool out of you, and now their making a fool out of me. I need to know who this person is."

"I know you're supposed to be my sister-in-law, and blood is supposed to be thicker than water, but I can't tell you anything. Too much is at stake here."

"Fuck your little street code Omani. I guess that is the only code you abide by. Why did you have to bring me into this shit? I'm not getting a check for this shit. I didn't give anybody permission to do this so you had to. This is your entire fucking fault and you owe me some kind of explanation?"

"I don't know anything about no magazine cover or no photographs, and what I know is what I know. Snitches get stitches and I'm not getting any stitches for you."

"Whatever, Omani I'm so done with you. I promise you I'm going to find out who did this and when I do you better pray that you aren't in the crossfire because if you are consider yourself good as dead." Passive hung her phone up as fast as she could before she launched it into the wall like a baseball and broke it permanently.

Omani knew exactly who was fucking with Passive, but knew better then to snitch. She had no idea Lindsay took pictures of the shit though, even though Lindsay swore she knew that Omani was not fibbing about the kiss that struck between Passive and her, this was exactly what she needed. One of those proofs to bring Passive down.

Ready to go on an outrage, Passive decided to keep her blood pressure down and try to act like she never got that envelope or kissed Omani. She burned the envelope and all of its contents outside in the backyard. She kept telling herself this was just some kind of sick joke. Somebody was just trying to get to her. Somebody had nothing to do with their time but try to manipulate her life.

Chapter 9:

Gossip Girl

Gossip Is For People Who Don't Matter, Because People Who Mind Don't Gossip...

After yanking open the long black drapes over their house windows and allowing some sunshine to reflect its rays through their home, Passive got on the move to run her well-needed errands and spend some money. Shopping was the best and only antidote Passive ever used to cope with excessive stress. Since it was Friday, she had to get her end of the week massage. Maybe a massage was exactly what Passive needed right now to soothe her nerves. Unluckily, her and her cousin Charlene went to the same damn spa. Charlene made sure she got her massage on the same day and same time as Passive every week. Full of gossip, all Charlene ever did was talk Passive to death about her marital problems which was a big no-no for Passive. What goes on in your household should stay in your household.

Passive was trying to blend in with the rest of the women at the Woodhouse Day Spa, but her camouflaging technique was very unsuccessful because most of the women there were all white. Passive and Charlene were the only two black oddballs. Unfortunately, Passive had to stick with this spa because it was the only 5-star spa in her driving radius that she trusted and hasn't gone out of business yet unlike every other business in Detroit. It wasn't the gossip that got to Passive because white people gossiped too, it was Charlene that got on Passive's nerves, always messing up her peaceful time with her bullshit, but whether Passive listened to the white women or Charlene she

132

was screwed.

"Passive how's life been treating you?" Charlene greeted Passive as they got a pedicure and a foot massage. The Chinks must've hated Passive too because they sat Charlene right by her every single time.

"Good Charlene please don't make this day all about Mellow. Just sit next to me and shut up."

"Damn Passive why do you have to be so blunt?"

"Being blunt would be me saying that I wish I had some duct tape so I could duct tape your mouth shut." Passive wished she had some headphones or earplugs so she could really tune Charlene out, because just trying to relax wasn't helping.

"Well fine let's talk about the tramp they then hired at the precinct. Did Smoke tell you about her because you know Mellow told me about the bitch?"

"I already know about the tramp. Shouldn't you be worried about if that's the bitch that got you and Mellow getting a divorce?"

"No, why would Mellow cheat on me with some bitch at his job?" Even though Passive was wrong to be putting bugs in Charlene's head after everything she was going through herself, she just wanted Charlene out of sight and out of mind. It wasn't her fault that Charlene was so damn gullible.

"Why wouldn't he? He gets to see the bitch every day, have lunch with her, sneak off with her, and do all of that lovey dovey shit he use to do with you."

"Yeah you right I never thought about it being some bitch at his job. I always assume he's going to cheat on me with some cheap hooker or some pole swinging hoe."

"You just goin sit there? Girl you better go get your husband's mistress. I think that bitch name Shania too." Just like that by getting in Charlene's head who was obviously easily persuaded and kind of on the slow side she got her gone. Charlene was so amped up she was about to leave without paying, in just the parlor's bathrobe, but she couldn't leave without her belongings or paying because the Chinks were about to be doing karate, tai-kwon-do, and saying "you pay", "we call the police" or whatever else they had to say in their broken English to get paid, but Charlene didn't want to get banned from her favorite parlor so she paid the money and was out.

Charlene got to the police station in 5.5 seconds freeway time, maximum speed raising cane. Funny she would be breaking the speed limit so horribly when her husband was a law enforcer, but Charlene always used her husband's connections to get out of any police trouble.

Boldly Charlene led herself all the way to Mellows' desk.

"You've been fucking around with that new bitch haven't you Mellow? Where is the bitch?" Charlene scanned around to detect Shania.

"I want to see the bitch that you've been cheating on me with. That bitch better not be hideous either."

You would think police would be all over Charlene escorting her dramatic ass out of the building or threatening to lock her up if she didn't mellow down, but it wasn't anybody in the precinct, but a whole bunch of black men who loved drama and wanted to see a chick fight, and a husband and wife fight to.

"Baby come on we do this enough at home why we got to do this at my job? Why are you putting all of our business out on Front Street? I don't come to your job and put all of our business in the street. Haven't you heard of the saying what goes on in our household should stay in our household?"

"You can't front me off at my job because I don't have one with your dumb ass. Where the fuck is this new bitch at anyways I'm about to give her a new face." Charlene took off searching for Shania and then she bumped into her coming out of the break room.

"Oh there you go bitch. I was looking for you so you like fucking people's husbands huh?"

"I don't even know your husband. Look at me don't it look like I got enough problems of my own." Shania answered.

"Yeah, but just because it's something wrong with your face don't

137

mean it's something wrong with your pussy. I was going to beat the shit out of you, but since someone has already done that I'm just going to leave you with a warning better yet a promise. You better stay the fuck away from my husband or else you'll find out." Charlene left with a quick sigh seeing Mellow and the rest of his army eavesdropping. They sure as hell didn't get in the middle of a mix-up with two women because if punches went flying and they were hit, they would have to roll with the punches, but compared to two angry niggas two angry females wasn't nothing even though females do fight dirty. Men don't fight at all no more, they rather settle their disputes or anger with gun wars.

Still Shania had to make herself look like the baddest bitch even though Charlene made her look as scary as a midnight shadow.

"Y'all better learn how to

control y'all women because the next
bitch that storms up in here accusing
me of fucking one of y'all, I'm going to
tell the bitch I did it, and give her
something and someone to be mad at,"
but the words that came out of
Shania's mouth was useless because
the men still were going to be her
suckers.

Chapter 10:

Never- Ending Disturbias

It's A Triple Treat And You

Don't Even Know It...

Joyful it was the weekend, Smoke and Passive felt like it had been centuries since they got some alone time together where they could put their love on top. They thought their home, and the weekend was safe from the three conniving people in their supposed to be devoted, married lives, but the triple threat June, Shania, and Omani were like never-ending disturbias who probably were related to Lindsay since they all seemed to have one distinct thing in common which was either to seduce Smoke or Passive, and destroy their happy home. Passive and Smoke were chilling back, watching the movie "Brown Sugar" on their big screen TV and eating homemade popcorn when Smoke's phone began ringing off the hook.

"You were expecting a phone call baby?" Passive asked not use to hearing Smoke's phone ring like a hotline especially not on the weekend during their alone time.

"Nope I don't know who this could be." Passive paused their movie so Smoke could answer his phone, and she could hear everything that was about to be said.

"Hello."

"Smoke it's an emergency I need you to come to my house now!"

"What? Is this Shania? How'd you get my number? I don't know where you live." When Passive heard Smoke say Shania's name you could've sworn her head spun around like the girl's head did on The Exorcist.

That little sneaky bitch don't know who she fucking with. I can't believe this bitch is calling my man.

Passive didn't know anything about Shania's alleged abuse, or Smoke asking her out to lunch.

"Please don't be mad, but Black gave it to me. I hope I'm not interrupting you," Shania started sniffling.

"No you weren't interrupting me, but what's the emergency?" Passive just knew Smoke wasn't about to leave her to play Mr. Comforter with Shania. Getting more and more flustered by the second she continued to listen to the man she married and was still married to talk on the phone to another bitch like she was invisible.

"I just got into another fight with my boyfriend."

"And you want me to come to y'all house?" Hoping Shania wasn't that dumb, and wouldn't disrespect her man like that even though her man was beating her ass he was still her man. And this was not Smoke's fight. He didn't want to be in the middle of nothing Shania had going on with her man. Her make-believe man anyway.

"No silly I was thinking we could meet up somewhere like a nice, dressy restaurant, I mean the strip by the Detroit River I just need someone to talk to right now before I go crazy. I'm the only child and I'm not exactly a fan when it comes to females. I wish I had somebody else to talk to, but I don't. All the other men we work with don't care anything about me they just want to fuck. Their just turned on by my sex appeal. You just didn't strike me like the type, see you got me fumbling over my words and imagining things I probably shouldn't be, but I can't help myself."

"Okay Shania just breathe. I'll be there just let me get dressed, and I'll call you right back." Shania was proud to catch Smoke off guard since he tried to play her on the date tip, and she definitely wasn't the weakest link when it came to love. Passive was just watching Smoke throw on some clothes.

"Are you serious Smoke?"

"Yes baby this is it- the day I can make the deal with her. I thought it was going to take longer, but with her boyfriend knocking her upside down on a daily basis- she is at a very vulnerable place."

"Maybe, but this bitch really likes you. She got your number and she got you running to her rescue. What's next? She's going to get our address and then she's going to pop up on our doorstep like you owe her some back child support or something? I will not pretend not to be your wife and that bitch isn't going to be getting comfortable up in here with you! Oh hell no! Have you forgotten you're supposed to be getting close to her, not her getting close to you stupid?"

"Well what do you want me to do Passive?"

"Cancel! Make her wait. You'll see her ass on Monday because this is my weekend and I'm going to spend it with you. Fuck what that bitch talking about."

"Alright baby I'm about to call her back." Smoke made up an excuse and told Shania he would have to postpone their little walk around the river for another rainy day. Of course Shania was highly upset seeing as though she had to call four out of six people just to get Black's number and she had to argue with two baby momma's, one mother, and two girlfriends even though all she really had to do was call Lindsay. And now all of a suddenly their plans were put on hold. Shania went on a rage after she got off the phone with Smoke starting in her dinette area. She sat down at her dining room table, opened up her China cabinet, and started breaking traditional dishes that had been in her family for generations everywhere one by one as each thought she had consumed her.

"All I wanted was to spend some time with him, but I'm not good enough to spend time with him." One dish hit the floor.

"All this shit I've been going through and doing just to get his attention and still he treats me like I'm invisible." Another dish hit the wall.

"Fuck this I'm not going to stop now I just got to get cleverer. I'm not waiting to Monday. I'm going to go visit this nigga at his house tomorrow. And just as Shania got his number she figured she will get his address." Shania threw another dish into the living room and shattered it into pieces.

****

Omani who was still thinking

146

about how shit just got real with Passive, was just lying in her bed in some Vickie Secrets as always when a couple of knocks came from her closed door.

"Come in." Omani knew it was none other than Onyx.

"Since I can't fuck anybody else in this bitch can I fuck you?" Onyx asked butt naked standing before her like a king with a rock hard body that could still make any woman faint.

"I didn't say you couldn't fuck anybody else, but I guess that's what my actions said huh?"

"Damn right, but right now I'm horny as you see and I know you horny so what do you say we fix this right here and right now?"

"Let's go then and let's see if you still got it."

"Hell yeah I do. We both know the real reason why you bi-sexual."

"You always talked too much."

Onyx slowly undressed Omani out of the garments she had on, then he bit his bottom lip and squeezed her ass cheeks a couple of times just thinking about fucking her again. As far as Onyx could remember Omani had the best pussy he had ever had. He just never wanted to give her credit for her sugar walls since they were broken-up, but now he couldn't resist temptation

Onyx got Omani's click wet, dripping wet with his exotic tongue vibrations and movements. Somebody had transformed Onyx from a regular twat licker to a professional head banger because he never got her wet like this before off his head. Onyx never had her riding his face, rubbing her clit, stroking his dick, and grabbing her breasts while he ate her for dessert before neither. Before Onyx broke his way into Omani's walls Onyx made his dick super soaker wet so he could make her come off three hard long strokes just like he did. What the hell was Onyx thinking though? He didn't come strapped, and didn't bother to pull out when he came. When he was fucking her, her pussy had him zoning back to the old days when he used to go up in her and made him fuck her harder, deeper, and faster. He was too busy daydreaming to even know he was coming. And Omani couldn't distinguish whether Onyx just had some good ass dick or it was only good because they both wanted a nut. Omani was in a trance though- a trance she didn't want to end not now- and not ever. Finally long, sweaty, never-ending hours later Onyx rolled over to chat with Omani before he went back to his room and reality set in.

"Onyx you came?"

"Yeah do you think I would be laying here on the side of you if I didn't? I bust three nuts to be exact why?"

"You didn't pull out?"

"You didn't stop me neither when I was fucking you. You were too busy screaming daddy, and don't stop I don't see what's the big deal it's just wasted sperm. Don't you take them birth control pills?"

"No I don't. I'm sorry it was my fault I'm just use to strap-ons and shit. I just got caught up in the moment, but I know that's not too hard to believe."

"Well let's not jump to conclusions. Let's just see what happens, but if you are pregnant we can be a family." Onyx made Omani feel extra geeked before he left. She couldn't believe her ears. She must have some wax in them.

Omani's feelings for Onyx were undeniable, and had her feeling some type of way. Only pregnant, dreamy, complete thoughts sprouted from the ceilings of her mind. She felt a little guilt to as too why anybody would want to be with a scandalous bitch like her. If Onyx knew all of the countless sins she has committed in the past couple of years, he would probably run and stay as far away from her as possible. If she was pregnant she was going to have a lot of relationships to repair, if they were even repairable. Pregnancy is supposed to be a period of maturity, calmness, happiness, and joy, but Omani's lifestyle was going to interfere with all those states of tranquility, until she had some heart to heart interventions with her old ways, and formed a new alliance that only included her and Onyx, and whoever else decided to forgive her.

****

Still Charlene and Mellow were beefed out over Charlene's newfound identity of his mistress. Yeah he had a mistress, but Shania wasn't it so he could either tell his wife the truth so they could finally move past his unfaithfulness or he could continue to be a couch sleeping husband until Charlene finally got over it and they made-up, but something had to give because even Mellows' kids were teasing him for sleeping on the couch.

"Go clean up your room Cherish," Mellow ordered his 4 and 1/2 year old daughter.

"Why should I have to clean up my room if you don't have to clean up yours anymore?"

"What did you say little girl?"

"But daddy why can't I clean up the living room like you? I want to sleep on the couch too."

"No you don't baby girl. Then you going to have back problems and I don't want my little beauty queen having any kind of problems like me," Mellow tickled Cherish, and sat her on his lap.

"I think mommy is going to stay mad at you forever daddy."

"No she's not because I'm about to talk to her right now and I bet not catch you snooping in the hallway. Go see what your little brother and little sister are doing while you at it." It's crazy the senses that kids have when it comes to their parents. Even a child could see it was something going on with her mommy and daddy even though she didn't know the facts it made Mellow feel kind of bad because Cherish obviously looked up to him and the picture that him and Charlene were showing her of a good relationship was as fake as a knockoff because Cherish knew how her parents were supposed to be and she knew how her parents use to be. She was too young to be confused, or ripped apart from either one of her parents so Mellow marched in to what was just Charlene's room he felt like.

"Baby look I'm tired of sleeping on the couch and all this sleeping in other rooms shit is really affecting our kids so I'm willing to tell you who my mistress really was so we can move on."

"Go ahead I'm listening." Mellow began walking over to the bedside so he could be next to Charlene, but she stopped him right in his tracks.

"No tell me from where you standing at that way when you tell on yourself you can get a head start from this ass kicking your about to get."

"I was cheating on you with Karana baby." Immediately Charlene stopped folding up clothes.

"I know you're not talking about Karana from Sphinx? Isn't that the girl that danced at Smoke's bachelor party?"

"How you know that?"

"Karana is always in

somebody's gossip and plus we go to the same hair salon. That bitch was talking about Smoke's bachelor party like it was the Grammy Awards or something."

"I haven't fucked with her in over a year baby and I don't want too. I realize now that you and the kids are important to me and I will not lose y'all to some popcorn hoe. I swear I will not do anything else to jeopardize y'all happiness." The way that Mellow was talking and thinking made Charlene soften up. Hell she cheated on him too, even though it was after he cheated, it still didn't make things right especially not to be so infuriated with a man who was admitting to his mistakes and was willing to change for the sake of his good life.

"Okay you don't have to sleep on the couch anymore, but soon as I see Karana- you already know it's going down. I apologize for confronting that Shania chick, but I don't apologize for coming to your job. Shit you already knew I was crazy before you married me. So is that Shania girl kicking it with somebody at your job?"

"She say she got a boyfriend, but I personally think she's crazier then you because I don't know any nigga that would beat on a girl like that."

"So what are you saying?"

"I think she made all that shit up about the boyfriend and everything, but low key I think she likes Smoke."

"I better tell Passive next time I get a chance."

"Somebody better tell her before it's too late." Just like a couple to make up and then lie up in the bed and fixate on somebody else's problems like they don't have enough problems of their own.

******

That psychotic girl Shania was

really testing her luck. She lowered herself to bended knees by her bedside and began praying to God for answers on how she could possibly get Smoke's address without trailing blindfolded down the path of her co-workers again.

"Dear lord, please open up my mind to be intelligent in this journey that my heart and soul is leading me on. I have so many questions that I know you have the answers too, and who better to come seek encouragement and inspiration from then you. I hope the ways I am going about seeking this incredible man I want to be in my life aren't disappointing, but this is not a free world, and if you want something you got to go for it and that is exactly what I am doing. I am doing what I have to do to get what I want. I am doing what it takes to guarantee my happiness; a happiness that is long-deserved so at least I know that you can agree with

my strength and courage if you don't
agree with anything else, but lord
knows what all of this is going to come
too so let me just ask for your
forgiveness now before I get ahead of
myself..... Amen"

Shame on Shania, she knew damn well her ethics were nowhere near godly or Christian. Out of all the things God condoned, none of them included obsession. If she was going to ask anybody what she should do in this situation- she should've been consulting with the devil because he would be the most cognitive advisor in this sticky situation. It was no way for Shania to look Smoke up online or anything because she didn't know Smoke's whole name, or if Smoke was just a nickname or not, or any other bit of information like birth date that would help her find him the un-co-worker way because all Smoke's police badge said was "Smoke" so she decided to go ahead and call somebody who knew- who certainly wasn't a co-worker.

"You better have something good to tell me." Lindsay, Smoke's ex-lover answered.

"Not yet Lindsay, this whole process is slow motion, but I probably will have the news you want to hear if you give me Smoke's address."

"What the fuck do you need Smoke's address for? I'm the only person that needs to know that."

"Because this whole trying to get Smoke the nice way, your way isn't working so we need to start doing things my way. And I'm going to go to his house and see how his wife likes that. A woman visiting the house is sure to be a cheating eye-opener. I already got Smoke's number without you and called him. We had arrangements for a date, but Smoke canceled. He didn't even tell me he has a wife yet, but trust we will have plenty of time to get acquainted once I pry him away from Passive."

"That's exactly what kind of thinking I want to hear Shania. I know I will never have another chance with Smoke, but long as he's not with Passive that's all that matters to me," so Lindsay gave up Smoke's location hoping to be one step closer in her shady mission.

******

Instead of enjoying the rest of her weekend with her man, Passive was in a Shania frenzy. Passive could tell that Shania wasn't just going to accept their peace offer; she was going to negotiate her way up the ladder until she was satisfied because she was already pitching the balls with Smoke. Her main concern was if Shania knew about the drug exchange and was going to blackmail them or if she was just straight up digging Smoke and wanted to forever be his lady.

Smoke and Passive were still relaxing when another interruption came, but this time it was the doorbell. Passive and Smoke were actually expecting the pizza man from Jet's Pizza though, who had the best pizza in town to them, but Passive had just hung up the phone with Jet's Pizza like ten minutes ago. And everybody knows it takes an hour to deliver pizza whether it's right down the street from you or not. It couldn't be Jet's Pizza at the door. It would be nice if it was, but it wasn't. So who was it? Something told Passive to get up and open the door, but Smoke beat her to the punch.

"I'll get it baby." Smoke grabbed his white tee and put it on as he was strolling towards the door. He looked out the peephole first, but hoped his eyes were playing tricks on him when he saw that it was Shania. Now he was really confused on how she was getting his personal info and why she was trying so hard. She did not ever strike him as the desperate type until now. It was no way in hell Smoke could open that door right now. Passive had already put her foot down about if Shania ever tried to walk these walls, and Smoke couldn't let Shania find out he had a wife yet even though she already knew, so Smoke eased on back to the bathroom once he saw that Shania realized it wasn't nobody home. Smoke silently thanked man for inventing a garage.

"Who was at the door Smoke?" Passive asked in the hallway almost startling Smoke.

"Baby can I lie to you just this once?"

"What do you think?"

"Okay it was Shania."

"I know you didn't just say Shania? How the fuck did she find out where we live? You must've had this bitch in our house! I can't believe you would bring a bitch to our house! This is supposed to be our house! I bet even Elmo knows where we live! What the fuck is going on with you and that bitch? First, she's calling you now this? I know you've had to do something to that bitch for her to be on our doorstep!"

"Nothing is going on. This girl is fucking with me. She is fucking with us. I didn't give her my number. I don't know hers, and I didn't tell her or show her or even give her any inclination about where we live. I haven't even had a real conversation with the girl yet off of work time."

"You told her to fuck off?"

"No I didn't answer the door that way she is not sure who really lives here."

"Well what the fuck are you going to do because I know you got me fucked up now Smoke for real.

You got bitches calling your phone and coming to our house? What the fuck am I supposed to think? I know all the blame doesn't just go to that bitch and if it does you better show me before I leave your ass."

"I promise I'm going to turn this around on Monday if it's the first thing I do." Smoke tried to redeem himself even though Shania kept building a bigger and deeper well for him to fall through.

Chapter 11:

Fortune Teller Words

Advice Is Advice No Matter

Where It Comes From...

Usually Monday mornings were refreshing, but today Monday was go ham Monday because Smoke was going to arrange a meeting excluding Shania from it and go ham on all of his male co-workers soon as he got to work. He woke up and left early to avoid Passive because he knew he was on her bad side so until he was on her good side again he had mine as well distant himself from her because being on Passive's bad side was worst then knowing a fake person because at least they speak to you. Passive probably wasn't going to speak to Smoke, look at him, or let him lay a finger on her- none of that. She was going to treat him like he didn't even exist until he made everything better.

On Smoke's ride to work he was putting the pieces together to the puzzle. The only people that Smoke could quickly blame for Shania's indecent behavior is the men at their precinct since they were the only people that he knew off rip had a close acquaintanceship with Shania and could be easily manipulated by her even though they were just one part of the scenario. When Smoke got to work he was ready to rip every single cop at his job a new asshole. He made a brief statement on the intercom system at 8:30aam sharp which left the whole precinct shook.

"If you have a badge and you're a cop, please meet me in the conference room ASAP. Today there's going to be some layoffs."

Of course Shania heard that fine, sexy voice over the intercom too, and automatically figured the meeting was going to be touching issues about her.

"Since we're all grown men and I am the captain I'm not going to beat around the bush with y'all loudmouth motherfuckers. Y'all had y'all turn to talk now it's mine. This meeting is basically about Shania who seems to have a big crush on me. Most of you are stuck on stupid over her, but I'm not, and I don't appreciate you guys giving out my personal information to her no matter how she drags it out of you, my personal information is not to be given to her or anybody in this building period. It seems I have been getting phone calls and a visit from her to my house which is very inappropriate seeing as though I have a wife and you all should know that Passive isn't having that bullshit and now I'm in the doghouse because of what one or more of y'all then said. I'm not going to point no fingers in this bitch, and I don't even care who said the shit no more, but all I know is if Shania finds out any more information from any one of you guys about me, I'm going to put my foot in one of y'all asses and mess up y'all happy homes like y'all fucked up mines." Everybody was just looking around like they were lost and didn't know what the hell Smoke was talking about.

"Is that understood?"

"Yes boss." All the suited up men in the meeting agreed in unison.

"Alright now get the fuck out of here quietly and get back to work." Sitting in his office chair with his feet elevated on the desk Smoke solved one problem, but he still had a couple more to go before he could actually live his life peacefully again. Next problem he figured he would solve would be June, but it was too early to call so he waited.

Smoke put the D in dirty cop so he took off work for two days so he could go down to the dirty south himself and take care of the June he knew whether it was the June Passive was informing him about or not. Smoke didn't want his wife to go astray so he had to do what he had to do. Since Passive wasn't speaking to him, he decided he didn't need to call her, and let her know that he was about to leave town so he drove his black ass down to their house in Louisville.

*****

While Smoke was on the road transitioning himself from cop to killer, Passive decided to make some moves, not even thinking once about her husband Smoke or anything else tragic that was surfacing in her life. Every now and then, Passive let her mind take over her and partake in spiritual readings to re-cleanse herself from her problems and snap her back into her normal self. True or untrue, there was nothing like an outside opinion. The name of the smartass that kept Passive on her P's and Q's when she felt like losing it was Laura. And Laura was a middle-aged white woman who looked just like a white Erkyah Badu the way she dressed in long-flowing tribal dresses, and wore her hair wrapped up in a scarf high on her head. Laura was the only person Passive felt could help her in the mental state she was in so she whipped her up something quick in the kitchen while watching the weather channel to get an overview of the day's partly sunny weather. Then she showered, got dressed, hopped in her ride, and headed for Redford Township.

Passive hadn't seen Laura in about 3 months, which was the last time her and Smoke got into an ugly argument and she was thinking twice about her drug dealings, but Laura revealed that there is no other man that is in Passive's future besides Smoke, and that their drug dealings are safe as long as they keep their a-game tight which weren't in her fortune teller words, but close enough. Not to mention Smoke had no idea that Passive would trust their secrets within a psychic he would probably have a million things to fuss about if he knew anything about Laura.

All Passive did was walk-in, there was no direct eye contact at all. Senselessly, Laura's spiritual gifts picked up on her presence and she told her to take a seat. Nobody paid Laura like Passive did. Passive was happy though she could be seen right away. Usually Laura kept people running in and out of her candle-lit, dark-colored, and beady sanctuary because inquiring minds wanted answers.

"Come sit down and let me see what's been bothering you." Laura closed her eyes shut and swirled her hands around her magic globe, and then placed her hands on Passive's open, shaky palms.

"..... I see you and your husband haven't been getting along lately because of some new girl who has her tiny eyes on your husband and you're mad at your husband because you think he is cheating on you......"

"Yes...." Passive agreed in awe of Laura's gift.

".... Well Smoke is still as loyal to you as he's ever been. But this new girl I see she plans to cause you a lot of pain and grief among others.... but there is a mastermind behind your marital and life circumstances and that is who you need to look out for... this woman is not a stranger neither... She is someone in your husband's past... And... and..."

Laura's light brown eyes widened and she started hesitating which meant she saw something unbelievable and Passive had to know

what it was. Passive knew it was
something big; something terrible.
Never had Laura acted like this before
whenever Passive sat before her.

"Please tell me Laura."

"I don't want to. You don't have
to pay just go."

"Come on I will give you 1,000
g's right now if you just tell me. I need
to know. Please!" Passive begged
feeling alarmed; feeling a sudden
danger come over her life.

"It's not about the money. I've
known you for a long time and I'm
looking out for you right now by not
telling you. I don't know how well you
can handle what I've seen."

"Let me be the judge of that."
Passive dug in her purse and pulled out
nine hundred dollars. Usually she paid
Laura a hundred dollars every time,
but she felt the need to give her a nine
hundred dollar bonus to get what she
wanted. As far as she was concerned

money was everybody's first language. If this didn't work then Passive was just going to settle for her free session and leave.

"...Okay your husband is about to commit a crime.... A crime that I know you condone... And will not detest... He's about to kill someone over you... and that woman that is working so hard to make your life a living hell is going to try to kill you when the time is right....and that's all I'm going to say..." Passive couldn't believe her ears. She wished Laura could tell her more, but she knew that wasn't going to happen especially about this woman. Smoke was obviously the only person that could help Passive with this no brainer, but he was on the road to kill. And Passive knew that the person her husband was about to kill was June. It made complete sense, but before she thought the worst, she had to check and see if

Smoke was at work so she called his job. And just like she figured Mellow told her that Smoke took off for the day. And as she could recall Smoke reassured her that he would handle it, and he would handle everything. Passive definitely wasn't angry anymore she was sad, and just wanted to be able to see her husband again so she went straight home, and hoped that he would make it back to her as always. She even called his phone and left him message after message telling him that she wasn't mad at him anymore and she just wanted him to come home as soon as possible, but she just kept getting the voicemail. And it was the last time that she knew that Smoke wasn't going to return until he killed, until he did what he felt he had to do, what needed to be done, and Passive was starting to understand that and was awaiting the return of her superman wondering how could she ever doubt her husband's love for her.

******

When Smoke reached Louisville it was on. He didn't even bother to go to him and Passive's Louisville home because he wasn't planning on sticking around after his stick-up. He came here to do one thing and that's what he was going to do. His first stop was at a payphone where he called June from to try to set up a surprise meeting.

"Hello..." June answered wondering who the hell was calling him from an unknown number which payphone numbers were listed under.

"June this is Smoke I just got in town and I need to meet with you right away. It's about business as usual and I really need to get this squared away with you immediately. And don't worry I have a lot of good news to tell you." Of course Smoke's call caught June off guard but, they were still in business together and it was no telling what the meeting was concerning. It could be putting more bread in her pocket so it wasn't any way she could refuse.

"Where do you want me to meet you at?"

"Meet me downriver at our dock." Lucky June and Smoke had a couple familiar meeting places that were secluded which made it perfect for exactly what Smoke had in mind, but the thing that made it most perfect was that June wasn't going to see none of it coming.

"Alright I'm on the way." Smoke wasn't that many minutes away from the dock so he decided he would sit in a spot close to the dock where he could see June pull-up and once June left his car that's when he was going to exit his vehicle. Twenty minutes passed, and Smoke saw June strolling towards the dock looking just like a nigga so Smoke loaded his PERSONAL gun and put it into his gun-belt. Startling June who was all caught up in the downriver view, Smoke pressed his silver piece against her skull quickly. She couldn't move, she couldn't look, she couldn't think, but she was brave enough to talk.

"What is this about Smoke?"

"This is about you. I heard you've been harassing my wife-Passive- or should I say Diamond."

"Look I just seen her around town a couple of times, but I didn't know she was your wife." June lied. And Smoke clicked his gun.

"You're lying and I know you're lying!"

"Trust me you don't want to do this. I'm not the person you really want. I know the person you really want." June was just about to snitch on Lindsay until Smoke pulled the trigger and June's body fell back into the river she was just so amazed by.

"....Times up..." Smoke thought.

"I got to get home to my wife... It's not my fault he wanted to spend his last words lying. Maybe I would've spared her some more time if she would've been woman enough to admit the truth to me."

******

While June's body was sinking to the bottom of the river, Lindsay was calling her which was going to be bad for her name when the police finally found June's body if they ever found her body and checked her phone records. And June's not answering her phone made Lindsay kind of uneasy so she decided to call Omani next especially since it seemed like her team was playing horseplay with her money. Lindsay wanted to hear about progress, but the only thing she was hearing was herself thinking until

Omani answered her phone that is knowing that it was about time she had her "bitch fuck you" talk with Lindsay.

"Hello." Omani answered calmly while Onyx was almost finishing taking a hot, refreshing shower.

"Omani what the fuck is going on with our operation? I don't feel like y'all bitches doing shit, but sitting on y'all flat asses and waiting for something to blow up in your face! What the fuck don't you bitches understand? I paid y'all to destroy their marriage not keep it together!"

"What the fuck is going on with your operation you mean? And what do you mean you bitches all I know about is me and what you asked me to do. It ain't shit going on with your operation because I want out. I don't even know why I agreed to do this shit because it's stupid your stupid and I quit!"

"You can't quit shit. I paid you for your services, and I want my monies worth. So either your going to give me all of my money back or I'm a beat that shit out of you until the damages on your body equal up to your debt!"

"Try me Lindsay. I really don't think you want to step to me because I got enough information about you to put your ass up under a cell!" Lindsay drew the phone back and looked at it in awe. She couldn't believe little old Omani was trying to get all bossy with her.

"You must be on your period or something because I know your young ass ain't tripping on me like this after all the shit I've done for you? Bitch I made you!"

"What have you done for me but make my own brother and his wife have reason to hate me!" Just as Omani was finishing her sentence,

Onyx was coming out the shower, and was a couple seconds from snatching the phone away from her.

"Do you honestly think they give a fuck about you?"

"Ain't nobody bout to have my woman yelling at the top of her lungs like this. So if you got something to say to her you need to say it to me because I forbid her from speaking to your ass anymore." Onyx spoke very manly.

"This don't have shit to do with you homeboy, but check this out I hope you and Omani got an escape plan over there because y'all got less than ten minutes to get the fuck out of there before I come for both of y'all heads. Click..." Lindsay wasn't bullshitting about the threat she had just made neither, but Onyx who was dressed in nothing but a towel, was lost.

"Omani Sade Mitchell you

better get to talking right now."

"I don't have time to tell you what's going on. I'm sorry I got you involved in this I just can't do this anymore, but we have to go right away!"

"It's okay baby. I don't know what you got us into, but I can tell this is not a good time to ask questions let's go." With nothing but a towel on, and Omani with nothing but a robe on, a sexy nightgown, and house shoes abandoned their apartment swiftly. As they were going down on the elevators almost to the main floor, Lindsay's two hit men were on their way up on the elevators to the fifth floor.

Chapter 12:

It's A Woman's World

Women Rule But No Reign

Goes Without Disparity...

Returning to work was everything, but thrilling to Smoke, except he was happy he disposed of the disloyal "June". Smoke knew if his scheming was going to continue to work, his blood was not going to be on Shania's hands. There was no way he was going to sucker Shania or himself into becoming a team player especially not on the verge of losing Passive. Evidently, Shania was already showing early symptoms of destruction, and Smoke hadn't even put his Love Jones on her yet totally, so he decided he was going to have to do his thing solo especially since some of his other drug contacts were hungry for more. The only thing he could hope for was that he wasn't going to have to be the thief and the transporter, and that Passive would continue to do her part despite her reasonable anger. Hopefully Passive would be relieved when Smoke re-informed her about how things had to be handled, and she wouldn't doubt Smoke one bit, but women are so unpredictable, Smoke's new ways probably weren't going to be enough.

Since "June" was now 60 feet under, all Smoke and Passive had left was four main contacts who were all ladies by the way simply because it was no longer just a man's world it was a woman's world too when it came to drugs. Women loved money just as much as men, more than men if you really want to be honest, and women loved to get money by any means long as they weren't tricking. The oldest of the duo's contacts was Champagne, and the youngest was Paradise and the other two were Neiva and Sunrise.

And the four of them were pressuring Smoke about their sudden urgency to re-up and tonight he decided he was going to pay another visit to Shania's dungeon.

*****

Still Onyx and Omani were on the run like two convicts, and were hiding-out like two smart mice who knew there were open mice traps out. Of course, Omani didn't have any family besides Smoke, but how could she turn to him after what she was trying to do to him and his marriage? In his eyes she would be just as guilty as Lindsay, and untrustworthy. He would probably never ever forgive her this time. Even though, being so close to him on the eastside made her want to cling to him more and more, she knew he wouldn't give her open arms. Luckily, Onyx had plenty of family and his cousin Luis and girlfriend Lacy agreed to let them stay there in their newly- remodeled 5-bedroom humble home for as long as they needed until they could figure things out, but Onyx and Omani didn't want to stay anywhere for longer than a week.

Lacy and Luis were just too argumentative for Onyx and Omani. Every day, every hour on the dot as a matter of fact they was always arguing about something. Lacy would pick the stupidest things to argue about, while Luis would make the stupidest comments during the argument. Not even Dr. Phil could help these two with their boyfriend/girlfriend difficulties, but all that arguing just wasn't healthy. Omani and Onyx would even try to tune them out with the TV or the stereo, but somehow they would only manage to get louder and louder and more obnoxious.

Omani knew she would have to tell Onyx everything about her partnership with Lindsay and when the time was right she was going to spill the beans. Hopefully, he would understand that money and deception was all that Omani knew and was in her character, and that only he had the power to change that. And it was obvious Omani wanted to change, because she told Lindsay she quit. Whatever they was going to do though they had to think of something quick because it was no way Onyx was going to be on the run forever. They knew it was going to be pointless to go to the police because it would be months before they could develop a case against Lindsay and arrest her, it was no point of starting over elsewhere because their problems with Lindsay was never going to go away, so the only sensible thing left to do would be to go after Lindsay and give her a taste of her own medicine, and just like Lindsay had a team to destroy Smoke and Passive, Onyx and Omani was

going to need a team to destroy
Lindsay so Omani was just going to
have to have suck it up and tell her big,
bad brother before it was too late.

*****

Back at Onyx's and Omani's
old apartment were the two men
Lindsay hired to chop their heads just
laying around on the couch chilling,
with their big ass feet stretched out on
the coffee table, guns laid out on the
kitchen counter, smacking on some
microwave popcorn, watching music
videos checking out all the video girls
waiting for somebody to turn the key
in the door and try to get some of their
belongings. Little did Lindsay know
they were getting paid for nothing
because neither Onyx nor Omani was
ever going to return to that apartment,
and the two men Lindsay hired mine as
well just die there.

Bang! Bang! Bang! The two
guys Kirk and Kurt could barely hear

the loud knocks that were coming on the apartment door since they had the TV volume super high so they put the TV volume on mute to make sure their senses weren't playing games with them and they wasn't.

"Open up it's the landlord or I will use my key!" The landlord threatened.

"I know y'all in there! Y'all know what time it is! Y'all shouldn't have had the TV up so damn loud if y'all didn't want anybody to know y'all wasn't at home!"

Usually around rent time the landlord would give all of his occupants a personal reminder he wanted his money. Kirk and Kurt didn't know what to do after hearing the landlord was going to barge in to the apartment and drop off his rental notice on the coffee table. Forget sliding it up under the door, sticking it on the door, or sticking it in the mailbox, Mr. Waters preferred to have a brief, face to face conversation with his tenants about the rent to let them know he meant business. Kirk and Kurt were only hired to blaze Omani and Onyx. And they sure wasn't about to kill nobody for free, without no extra cut in their pockets before the kill so they were frozen until they glanced at their guns spread out on the kitchen counter. They knew they had to hide their weapons before Mr. Waters entered, but their time was running out because Mr. Waters was already on the second key and the top lock. By the time Mr. Waters opened up the door Kirk and Kurt had planted their weapons away and flopped back on the couch.

"Who the hell are y'all and where is Onyx and Omani?"

"They went out of town, were their cousins and were just house-sitting while their gone you know

191

doing the type of stuff house-sitters do; check the mail- water the flowers- etc." Kirk lied instantly making Mr. Waters suspicious because as he looked around the house all he saw was 3 large fake plants, and as for the mail they had a mailbox to let their mail pile up in.

"Well I hope they left y'all the rent money because if they didn't they already know I will put their ass out on the curb."

"Yeah they left it, it's no problem."

"Alright then that's all I wanted and turn that damn TV down in the meantime."

Kirk and Kurt were relieved when Mr. Waters left. They figured they wouldn't even tell Lindsay about the money hungry landlord, and they would keep it to themselves. Hopefully they wouldn't have to spend no more than two more nights sleeping in

Omani's apartment because if they had to spend any more nights there they were definitely going to have to pay the rent to keep Omani's apartment in their hands.

******

Finally Smoke felt it was time to steal some more drugs. Usually Smoke would be at home at this time with his wife, but why would he want to be there when he had money on the floor, and she was giving him the silent treatment so Smoke worked overtime. Nobody was really in the precinct besides three other cops and Shania so down to the evidence room Smoke went. Shania could smell Smoke's favorite cologne which was Sean John's fragrance "I am King" heading towards her way before she even seen him coming so she prepared herself to apologize, but she would've been better off keeping her mouth shut.

"I'm sorry Smoke for how I've

been acting lately. I had no right to invade your privacy and your life the way I've been doing. I don't know what I've been thinking."

"It's okay. I have a strong woman beside me. I'm fine and my life is fine."

"So do you think you could ever forgive me?"

"Yeah you're forgiven just like that. I don't like to hold grudges. I know you're probably getting sleepy though so would you like a cup of coffee?"

"That would be great."

"I'll be right back." After Smoke made Shania a deadly cup of coffee, he looked around to make sure he was clear, than he reached in his pocket and pulled out a couple pills of Sonata whose generic name was Zaleplon. He stirred the coffee excessively and let them dissolve in the dark, black substance. Smoke didn't even care about the dangerous side effects of Sonata, or the fact that it was for sleep-deprived people, and it wasn't for everyone. Money was on his mind, and money was about to put Shania into a long sleep goodnight.

"Here you go." Smoke handed Shania the coffee.

"Where's yours?"

"Oh I don't drink coffee, I drink tea. I forgot mines upstairs." Smoke lied.

Smoke stood there and made small talk with Shania until she dozed off then he went in for the steal and took four connects worth of drugs in duffel bags, and hauled them out to his car before anybody could notice.

Chapter 13:

Side Effects

Every Action Has A Consequence...

"Shania! Shania! Wake up!" Officer Black shook Shania gently at her post trying to prevent her from getting written-up and even worst fired for falling asleep on one of the most important jobs in the precinct especially since all of Shania's long hair was covering up her face. This was the first time Black ever found Shania snoozing on the job, and he wondered if the night shift was suitable for her, or if there were other things going on in her life preventing her from getting necessary sleep. Unfortunately, Shania had been asleep for over 3 hours, and it wasn't no telling how long she would've stayed asleep if somebody hadn't tried to wake her up.

Shania woke up slowly feeling

dizzy, vision kind of blurry.

"What's going on?" Shania
asked barely able to tell where she was
at. Her nose started bleeding heavily.

"What's wrong with you
Shania? Are you drunk or something?"

"I don't drink, but I feel
horrible."

"Are you tired?"

"No there's definitely
something else wrong with me."

Next thing Black knew Shania
bent down to the round garbage can
that was up under her ledge and began
vomiting as the tart smell of throw-up
filled the air. And when Shania lifted
herself back up her throat looked
enormously bigger than usual. And
then Shania started talking funny
trying to say her tongue was starting to
swell. Then the need for oxygen
became very urgent for Shania as she
started having trouble breathing like
she was about to have an asthma attack

or something even though she had never had any problems with asthma or breathing beforehand so Black broke wind to call an ambulance that rushed the symptomatic Shania to the nearest hospital.

At Sinai Grace the staff at the hospital asked Shania a million questions, and ran a million tests on her. Each and every one of their results had a rush put on them to get down to the nifty gritty so they could identify the problem. Consequently, they informed her, they were going to keep her overnight even though she hated everything about a hospital- there was nothing she could do about it, but lay in her hospital bed with an IV in her arm, and eat hospital food. Black stayed there for a minute with her and kept her company, but then he went back to work shortly and spread the word about one of their finest being in the emergency room.

Since Smoke's shift was over
he figured he would fill Passive in on
her upcoming adventures so he called
her and told her to meet him at the spot
ASAP so she already knew what time
it was, but she didn't know, who was
the buyer this time, and where she
would be going, not until she got there
that is. Smoke was thrilled they were
making some kind of progress though,
because just a couple of days earlier he
couldn't even get Passive to think not
even a half of a thought about him nor
squint not even one eye at him. He
thought about informing Passive about
how Shania "the home-wrecker" was
in the hospital and he accidently put
her there, but he figured he would
spare her the details for now. Shit how
was he supposed to know that Shania
was going to have allergic reactions to
sleeping pills? It wasn't like she was
dead or anything.

Both Smoke and Passive reached their spot on Emily around the same time. Finally they kissed and hugged and showed each other some type of affection before they headed in the house to talk business. When they got in the house Passive was all ears. Smoke explained to her all the details about the trip which included the three buyers Passive loved delivering too. The fourth one Passive hated was the youngest one Paradise just because she gave Passive bad vibes and was a hothead. Since Smoke didn't want Passive to stay gone from him too long, and he felt like it was time he switched up their drop-points he changed things up a little bit something like double-travel. He would only let Passive travel to two different states instead of four, and when she would make the drop she would deliver double the work. The first drop was going to cover

Champagne and Paradise's end, and the second drop was going to cover Sunrise and Neiva's end so everybody was going to have to meet Passive halfway. And halfway was one stop in Chi-town, Illinois and another in St. Louis, Missouri.

Although, this time Passive didn't have an overnight bag, or wasn't going to have an extended stay away from her husband, she was glad Smoke planned out things the way he did considering all the mess that she encountered with June, but at the same time, she was kind of disappointed because whenever Sunrise, Neiva, Champagne, and Passive got together they were pretty much inseparable and loved to go out and wine and dine with each other. All Passive really needed for this trip though was her locations, her faith, and the drugs.

******

Through the grapevine,

Lindsay heard about Shania being in the hospital and she was beginning to think that trying to annihilate Smoke and Passive using a team was a big mistake, and if she wanted to get revenge on anybody she was going to have to do it herself so now she had to get rid of the team in case they turned out to be some real snitches which included Omani, Shania, and June who was already crossed off the list even though Lindsay didn't know that. And as much as Lindsay was about to try to kill Shania, her threat was really Omani because she was Smoke's sister and now her loyalty went to him.

Lindsay figured she would send somebody in to kill old Shania in her hospital bed and put her out her misery so Lindsay called the hospital to get Shania's room number, which was all Lindsay needed to send out her hit so she called upon this fellow named Reno to do her dirty job.

Once Reno got to the hospital he got a visitor pass, didn't look suspicious at all because he was dressed like a typical street thug in a denim pair of Levi's, a white t-shirt, shades, a leather jacket, and the latest 23's. It took him a couple of hallways and wrong turns to finally find the elevators, but when he found them he pressed the up button, and an empty elevator opened immediately. There wasn't nobody getting in the elevator with him thankfully so he could prepare himself for the kill he was about to make. His gun was intact, he turned his trigger happy self on, and was ready to dispose of the already disposable if they were a patient in a hospital. Usually if you were in the hospital most of the time that meant you was already dying or you were going to die.

As the elevators went up 2, 3 finally came 4, and Reno got off on the fourth floor. He saw that all the hospital employees on the fourth floor seemed to be keeping busy, and working in sync. He just moved through the fourth floor like an unnoticeable mime. He looked on the sides of the walls to read the room numbers since the walls always explained exactly where to go. And he saw the numbers for Rooms 400- 410 when he made a left turn so he kept straight. And was anxious to hurry up and find Room 410 BED A so he could pull the trigger.

Then he stood in front of Room 410. He looked at the second chart for BED B to see if there was someone else in the room, but lucky BED B was VACANT which meant his job was two times easier. He saw a chart that had Shania Davis scribbled on it so he figured he was at the right room so he entered it and locked the door behind him. Once he approached Shania's bed he pulled out his gun and put it to her head. "Damn it would've been easier if she was asleep," Reno thought to himself, but either way it went Shania was as good as dead.

"I swear if you scream, or try to push any button for help, it want matter, because by the time anybody comes in here you'll be dead, and I'll be long gone so put your hands up where I can see them. You look like a slick little something!"

"Why are you doing this to me?" The frightened woman asked laying on her deathbed without a clue why anybody would want to kill her.

But Reno didn't have any intentions on answering her. He was hired to kill not to answer questions so he pulled one of the pillows from behind her head, and gave her a bullet to the head. Nobody would even hear the bullet that just pierced the poor woman's skull because he had a

silencer on his gun and as quickly as
he shot her he continued to exit the
hospital and made it without being
caught. If only Lindsay and him
would've known that the woman he
just shot wasn't Shania. The lady was
named Shania Davis too just like
Shania, but it wasn't the Shania they
were looking for. It didn't even register
to the nurse to tell Lindsay that there
were two Shania Davis's present at the
hospital simply because it was only
one showing in the computer. The
damn computer just saved Shania's
life.

Chapter 14:

Free Will

We Choose The Life We Live...

Some secrets aren't meant to be kept, and family is always the first ones to expose you. That's exactly why you never shine a limelight on your insanity unless you are truly about that life and you are willing to wipe your whole family out if need be. Regardless of Lindsay's medieval plans, Marcela had some plans of her own and she didn't give a rat's ass where this broken trust would leave her and her sister because right is right and wrong is wrong.

Smoke Mitchell wasn't a hard man to get in contact with since he was a man who was suppose to uphold the law to the fullest extinct, so Marcela made her way to his precinct soon as she touched land in the D. Days of watching the Louisville local news, and reading the Louisville headlines, finally made Marcela have a revelation. That name Julie (June) Harris kept ringing bells in her head, even though she never knew June's whole name or real name she remembered the name June. She remembered the birthmark on her face that the news and papers described every time they reminded the city about the girl whose body was found shot in the Ohio River. She remembered that day at dinner with June and Lindsay, and Marcela could just bet her bottom lip that her deceptive sister had something to do with it. And she was not going to let anyone else's life be impacted by Lindsay's negative ways and her hatred for dear life so she bought herself a plane ticket to the D to pay an old friend a surprise visit.

When she arrived there of course she asked for Smoke and was instructed to sit in the waiting room until he called her to join him in a four-walled room in the back of the station.

It's been a hell of a long time since Marcela had laid eyes on Smoke, but she was more nervous about being a snitch, then being in Smoke's presence. Even though, police officers treat confessions like a walk in the park, they don't make you feel a sigh of relief once the shiny wrapper is unfolded. They make you feel like the epitome of society, like a snitch, dry snitching and shit just to walk around with a clear conscience. And it always seems like police officers will pull you over and write you a ticket in 30 seconds, but when you come in to do the right thing they make you wait forever in a stupid, sweaty lobby.

Finally the back doors of this god forsaken place opened and out came Smoke in his mighty uniform.

Marcela was not somebody that Smoke every expected to cross paths with especially not at his place of work. But at the same time he chose this life, and he wasn't in the position to turn away anybody unless he wanted to be without legit employment.

"Marcela what brings you here?" Smoke asked and led Marcela to the back. She already had the routine down packed in her mind.

"I have some disturbing news to tell you. Even though I hate to be the news-breaker, I can't let this information continue to go unknown." Marcela fidgeted and never let her eyes catch Smoke's eyes. She was that ashamed of her sister, and felt nasty sitting in a precinct for criminals, felons, and law-breaking citizens. In her mind she was too good for this low class shit.

"Do I need to get my pad and pen out?"

"No your concerns are more on a personal level and once I tell you what I have to say, you want forget one single word."

▪▪▪▪▪▪▪▪▪▪▪▪▪▪▪▪▪▪▪▪▪▪▪▪▪▪▪▪▪▪▪

Today was finally a day Lindsay could rejoice in, because the September issue of Dirty Raw was in stores everywhere. Cheating wives was one of the eye-catching subtitles on the front cover along with Omani Sade Mitchell and Passive Boone Mitchell's adjoined faces. Two beautiful girls, two beautiful sisters, with one scandalous story was finally going to give Lindsay the big break she needed in the entertainment sector of the world so her magazine could go from the 2nd best black-owned magazine to the 1st best.

Passive was in the outskirts of St. Louis when she pulled over at a BP gas station.

"Can I please get 40 dollars on pump 2," Passive asked the male BP cashier behind the counter. As the male was grabbing her money to put into the register, he couldn't stop staring at Passive very intensely.

"Do I have something on my face or something?"

"I'm sorry for staring so hard but you look just like this girl on the magazine on my shelf."

"I did a little modeling in my days, but I never modeled for a magazine before so you must have me confused," Passive hoped confusion was to blame for his identity mistake.

"I'm almost sure it's you," the BP cashier grabbed his magazine and showed Passive the front cover and there it was. There she was. Her worst nightmare was on the front cover of a magazine. The same magazine she burned in the backyard and hoped was some kind of a sick joke only there was no sick joke. This magazine was real. Dirty Raw was a real magazine, and she had to think fast because this magazine was already in stores all over the country. It could be minutes or seconds before Smoke got his hands on this magazine, or Smoke got word of mouth. Now it was time for Passive to speak up and out against the unknown so she bought a copy and ran to her car to call Smoke while she pumped her gas and rivers begin to flow down her chin.

"Baby I'm going to have to call you back, I have somebody in the interrogation room," Smoke answered.

"Smoke, I know your job is important, but you have to listen to me right now." Smoke did not like the sound of that. He knew it was something terribly wrong. What could have possibly went wrong now?

"What's wrong baby?"

"Do you remember that day when Omani came to the house on Emily and I kicked her out?"

"I remember that," Smoke said as he thought back.

"Well, your sister kissed me, and now the kiss, and me and her, are on the cover of a magazine. Some damn magazine that's in stores all over the country. Someone has been stalking me. Someone sent me pictures of me and her kissing to our house, sent me a devilish little letter, and a copy of this issue in an envelope addressed to Diamond Mitchell. Then I went to see a psychic when you went out of a town and she told me a woman from your past was going to try to kill me." Smoke couldn't believe his ears. He had no idea Passive even believed in psychics. He was shocked and upset at the same damn time, but he was also at work and on duty, so he had to be level-headed.

"Why are you just now telling me about this Passive? You should've told me about this the moment you opened up the envelope. I knew my sister tried something on you I just didn't know what. I'm sure she did this and she knows everything. Until we figure out what's going on I want you to come home. Let everybody know we have a delay. And when you get here come straight to the precinct, because I can't and I'm not going to let you out of my sight." Passive thought Smoke was going to kill her after she broke her silence, but he wasn't, or maybe he was just pretending to be receptive of everything. Either way it went he gave her specific orders, and with her life in jeopardy, she was going to follow them.

"I'm sorry Smoke, I love you."

"I know you love me Passive I love you too, please hurry up and get here." Derailed Passive made her way back to the D where it all began.

▪▪▪▪▪▪▪▪▪▪▪▪▪▪▪▪▪▪▪▪▪▪▪▪▪▪▪▪▪▪▪

Just minutes away from signing her hospital release papers, Shania's tests results were in, and her doctor was in to set the record straight.

"Mrs. Davis are you sure you were being completely honesty when we asked you if you were taking any prescribed medication?" Shania hated being questioned especially the one time in her life she was actually telling the forbidden truth.

"I was being completely honest I don't take any over-the-counter medicine?"

"Well in this case we found heavy traces of Sonata in your system which is a sleeping aid. You are allergic to Sonata and you were experiencing allergic reactions. If you would've come any later, or stayed asleep any longer you would've died in your sleep."

"Are you saying someone drugged me?"

"Yes, if everything you have told us is correct, you can't put anything pass people these days. Someone was just murdered in this hospital yesterday. Someone named Shania Davis also and she was a good patient of mine. I don't know anyone who would want to hurt her." Shania didn't know anyone who would want to hurt her either. She was positive nobody at her job wanted to hurt her. So who could it possibly be? Whomever the culprit was Shania didn't have time to let her mind ponder, but she was starting to feel very regretful.

Chapter 15:

Roger That

The Truth Only Sets You Free

From Dishonesty....

The stratus clouds in the puffy sky seemed like they were going to whoop down on Passive and wisp her away to heaven. Red was a horrible color especially for Passive who already had tons of anxiety from the multiple stress factors in her crazy life. Since Passive was instructed to call Champagne and Paradise and postpone their drug affairs she took her sweet little time at a Missouri traffic light to do so especially since it seemed like the light was never going to turn green. Right when Passive was about to enter the last digit to Champagne's number two black cargo vans had her squished in between them like they were trying to sandwich her. Out came 2 masked women in black masquerade ball masks, and 2 masked men in Aspen, Colorado ski masks and construction worker uniforms. The light was still red as Passive sat in her useless little Lexus as two Uzis were pointed at her head from two different severe angles and she was directed to roll down her window.

"Open the door bitch and get out!" One of the masked men ordered her in a low, affirming voice that sounded just like Barry White. Outnumbered Passive put her car in park and exited the vehicle with her hands up in the air. There wasn't enough space in between the vehicles for her to really move so she turned to her side and scooted all the way to the back of the van followed by guns and strangers. The back door of van#1 was already ajar for her to enter.

"Get in and don't make a sound," masked man#1 signaled with his gun, and as she was entering the van, he took her hands and handcuffed them behind her back like she was being arrested, as if he was mocking her husband's profession. Then they put a black pillowcase over her head and pushed her onto the van's floor like she was being held for ransom. The 2 masked women took off in her vehicle while the other van must've been trailing behind them as they took off to the point of no return.

This was complete madness how Passive's life was being obstructed by every unjustifiable force as possible. She knew this had to be a set-up because her and Smoke's enterprise was flawless. They didn't do business with small time drug dealers who were nickeling and diming through there hood letting customers get high on credit. They only did business with the best after the business prospects passed their pre-screening tests, but somehow they let a snake infiltrate their system. And it was only due time before that snake was found and buried.

••••••••••••••••••••••••••••••

Back at the precinct Smoke was about to go from a warm-hearted man to a serial killer.

"I'm ready whenever you are Marcela; I don't want to come off as an asshole but I don't have all day."

"Well I'm here to warn you about my sister Lindsay."

"What is your sister's deal? I'm really starting to think that it's something genetically wrong with all sisters these days. The last incident I had with your sister was when she crashed my graduation celebration." Marcela dug in her Michael Kors purse and grabbed her Louisville local newspaper that had Julie (June's) Harris face all over it with her rare facial birthmark.

"I am a witness to Lindsay hiring this woman named June to work for her in Louisville and now June is dead and I know that Lindsay had something to do with it." Smoke couldn't believe that he was looking at June's pathetic face on a newspaper. No murder goes undiscovered, but in this case Marcela was blaming Lindsay for everything. If only she knew who really put June out her misery.

"Why would Lindsay want to kill June and what was Lindsay hiring June to do for her?"

"Some details I cannot mention for your safety so I'm just going to use other words to explain it all. Somehow Lindsay found out about you and Passive's undercover work. The day she met June she found out that June did undercover work too and did this undercover work with Passive so Lindsay hired June to break up your marriage. Lindsay wanted to make

Passive fall in love with a stud since she knew that Passive would never cheat on you with a man."

"Is she obsessed with me or something?"

"Obsession is an understatement, and if I was you I wouldn't put anything pass her. If she would hire someone to break up your marriage it's no telling what she would do or wouldn't do for you or what she has done or hasn't done. All I know is you better keep a close eye on your wife because Lindsay is after her, and I don't want to watch the news and see her face all over it."

"I commend you for coming in here and telling me this information even though this is a total violation of trust."

"You know you were always a good friend of mine Smoke. There's no violation here I am only doing what's right. It's no telling how many lives are at risk here, and I would blame myself if something bad happened to your wife because of my sister."

"Well I must be going I did what I came here to do and I pray that you can stop my sister before anything else bad happens." Marcela left the territorial premises just as fast as she came.

It was extremely hard for Smoke to sit in that narrow, oppressive, and pride swallowing room and reverence on Lindsay, his traitorous ex-girlfriend, somebody he knew was a skeleton in his closet, but a closed chapter in his past, and her profound insanity. So after Marcela left he had a boxing match with the nearest wall launching punch after punch until his fists were without sensation. *This is fucking absurd. How one bitch is trying to mastermind my life and my happiness like she owns it.*

Lindsay is the last fucking person I would've ever thought would harm Passive. I can't believe I let this shit happen because if I would've never met that shady bitch, I wouldn't be dealing with this shit right now. I swear if anybody even lays a finger on Passive or brings a tear to her eye, they will never see the light of the day, and I'm going to make them suffer in the most excruciating ways possible.

■■■■■■■■■■■■■■■■■■■■■■■■■■■■■

Before Shania left her dreamless hospital parameters she realized that she was carless, purse less, and phoneless. She had to get a ride from somebody quick, fast, and a brisk hurry so she called her good friend Officer Rodgers. She got 411 to transfer her to the 11th precinct and then she got the 11th precinct operators to transfer her directly to Officer Rodgers.

"Hello this is Officer Rodgers speaking."

"Hey this is Shania, I just got released from the hospital and I wanted to know if you could come get me and give me a ride back to the precinct so I can retrieve my things and of course my car.

"You had us a little worried down here, but I'm glad to hear your okay so yes I'll meet you downstairs shortly. You don't need me to wheel you to the car or nothing like that right?"

"I see you got jokes, but I'm not handicapped. It's nothing like that Mr. Officer." Rodgers was flabbergasted that out of all the officers who worked at their precinct, Shania called upon him to come to her liberation.

Moments later, Officer Rodgers arrived under the hospital's valet parking viaduct fixed between its white lines and orange traffic cones. Shania got in the red, white, and blue squad car feeling thankful and lucky the more and more Sinai Grace Hospital disappeared out of her rearview mirrors. The closer and closer that Shania got to the precinct, the more she began to remember why she may have deserved for somebody to drug her, and the more she needed an outlet.

"Look Rodgers I don't know if I should trust you or not, but I'm going to take a leap of faith and trust you anyway because right now you're the only friend I have to confide in."

"You can trust me Shania we are all human you know. Everybody makes mistakes. Making mistakes is a part of life."

"Well I did a favor for a favor. This woman hired me to break up a marriage, as a favor for getting me this good old job I have. Come to find out when I was in the hospital someone was murdered there whose name was Shania Davis also. And the doctors tell me someone tried to drug me. I've been lying and conniving for a while. And I don't know what to do. If I tell the truth it's not a doubt in my mind that I will be fired on the spot." After Shania made her confession Officer Rodgers slammed on his brakes like he was trying to avoid a car accident.

"That's real fucked up Shania; I think you should get the fuck out of my car!" Officer Rodgers reaction was so unexpected, Shania couldn't believe her ears."

"I thought you were my friend Rodgers now your flip flopping on me?" It was mind boggling to Shania how Officer Rodgers could go from being a Samaritan to being a full fletched jerk.

"You don't deserve my friendship Shania. I felt bad for you on so many occasions. Its women like you that make it hard for men like me. Whoever is after you can stay after you, but I won't be caught up in your cross fire. This time I'm going to be smarter than that and use my head instead of my eyes." Shania didn't expect to lose a friend so quickly, but she was going to be walking on eggshells no matter where she went so she could either face the music or run from it. Mine as well face it because she was only a couple of blocks from her soon to be old job.

"What happened to everyone is human and everyone makes mistakes?" *I knew I couldn't trust him but at least I tried.*

"Our friendship is over Shania, I can't believe you would do that to Smoke. It's nothing you can say or do. Friends come before foes and you're a foe. So the sooner you close my door the sooner I can go." How did Rodgers know that Shania was indirectly referring to Smoke? Instead of continuing to look like a fool she slammed Rodgers passenger's door and he sped off. *I guess I should've just kept it to myself until I found Smoke and had a one on one talk with him myself.* Shania watched Officer Rodgers disappear down the same damn street she was about to began jay walking down. As long as she made it to her destination sound and safely that was all that mattered.

Chapter 16:

Fragile

How Can You Break Something

That Is Already Broken...

Smoke had been calling
Passive's cell phone nonstop like a
stalker to no avail from dusk until
dawn. Smoke who was ready to
massacre the whole world for his
beloved wife was still at his precinct
because it was the best place for him to
stay until he had a clear consensus of
what he was about to do. He had to
control his emotions even though they
were virtually uncontrollable.
Something had to give, Passive
should've been home by now right by
his side like the ride or die chick she
was. It had almost been 24 hours since
he last spoke with Passive, and
knowing that she was a target, he knew
something was dreadfully wrong. And
he knew that he was going to be the

one to fix it so Smoke figured the best thing for him to do was call his connects that Passive was supposed to be linking up with and see if he could get a lead on Passive from them. Just as Smoke was leaving an interrogation room, was trailing down the precinct hallways, and was about to exit through its gliding doors, someone began yelling his name.

"Smoke wait a minute bro I need to talk to you right away," Officer Rodger's yell echoed.

"I'm tired of talking and I'm tired of waiting to so whatever you have to say is just going to have to wait until I return," Smoke yelled back keeping straight on his path.

"It's about your wife Smoke," but at that point it was too late Smoke was already so far gone, and Officer Rodgers was so tuned out that it wasn't even no point of chasing him down.

On the way to Smoke's vehicle he came across a familiar face. Shania had been in the precinct and retrieved her things and she was just about to get in her vehicle and pull off before she told on herself.

"Shania you got released from the hospital?" Smoke asked walking up on her remembering what awful thing he did to her, but still not regretting it.

"Yeah I got released from the hospital today I didn't know you still cared," Shania answered as if she knew Officer Rodgers had told him her news, and as if someone had told her that Smoke is the perpetrator that drugged her.

"What do you mean if I still cared? Why would anyone want to see or hear that someone has been hospitalized?

"Right, but in all honesty I deserve everything that has and is coming to me and I'm fine with that."

"Is it something you want to tell me Shania because I'm not following you at all? You got me scratching my head."

"Smoke let me just confirm that Lindsay is after your wife and she is after me also. I called myself working for her and I was being paid to break up your marriage so if you hate me I totally understand."

"So everything that you were doing to me makes sense now. Why you came to my house, why you were always so overly flirtatious with me out of all these available men that work here you picked me?"

Smoke instantly grabbed Shania by the sides of her neck and hemmed her up against her car. "Well I have a confession to make too Shania I drugged you and that's why your ass was laying up in the hospital, but it looks like I should've drugged you more then what I did because you don't deserve to have a birth certificate bitch!"

"Smoke I'm sorry just let me go and I swear you will never see my face again."

"Bitch please, I'm not letting you go, your part of the reason why Passive is gone so you and everybody else that has something to do with her capture is going to pay."

"You don't have to do this Smoke, but I guess you mine as well because if you don't kill me Lindsay will finish her job."

"Lindsay is just going to shoot you, but me I'm going to make you suffer." Smoke took his left arm from Shania's neck still with a tight grip on her that wasn't going to be removed until he carried out his promise. He reached in his belt grabbed his knife, took his right arm off of Shania's neck and put it over Shania's mouth and turned her head to its side in the same motion that he moved her hair out of his way and he sliced her left ear, then turned her head to the other side and sliced her other ear off with no hesitation before Shania could even react to him it was already done. She was going to be deaf for life.

"Now you can live the rest of your life deaf bitch you will never be able to hear Lindsay coming for you or anybody. And now you can go back to the hospital and tell them somebody tried to kill you again, if you make it, and when they get you to write a report about who did it I know you better not say Smoke Mitchell." Smoke dropped her body by her car and kept it moving knowing damn well that would be the last of Shania Davis. Her car keys were still hanging loosely in her door so he grabbed those jingly jokers and tossed them into the sky fall.

He hopped in his car and was about to hit the road for Missouri.

▮▪▪▪▪▪▪▪▪▪▪▪▪▪▪▪▪▪▪▪▪▪▪▪▪▪▪▪▪▪▮

Still Omani and Onyx were cooling it under Onyx's people's protection. The only sunlight and fresh oxygen that they saw and felt was the light and air from the windows. Getting tired of living like prisoner fugitives, Onyx figured it was time to have that talk of declaration with his black angel Omani. Omani knew she was going to have to break her silence sooner or later so she didn't hesitate to open up about another one of her burdensome attempts that backfired in her face.

"So Omani what did you do this time?" Onyx asked with his strong arms of security stretched around her comfortable body.

"I made a deal with Lindsay Chambers, which is probably the worst mission I ever attempted to accomplish in my life."

"So Lindsay Chambers is the one who was on the phone and is gunning for our heads right now up and down Detroit?"

"That would be correct."

"And what exactly did this deal entail?"

"She was paying me to break up my brother's marriage, and she convinced me that Passive was deceiving my brother, but she wasn't. And she wanted me to turn Passive out, and I almost did, but I realize I couldn't go through with something like that." Onyx had to sit tall to finish this conversation because it was obviously putting him in an uneasy and upsetting place.

"Why are you always doing some hoe shit to your family Omani?"

"I know it was wrong Onyx, but the money was right. I didn't care about anyone but myself at the time, and I was strictly bisexual. Why wouldn't I want to catch a good girl on my hook? I honestly thought that she had betrayed my brother."

"Fuck money Omani there is nothing like family. I don't know who is going to hurt you more in this situation Smoke or Lindsay?"

"No one is going to hurt me Onyx. I don't want any parts to what Lindsay is or is doing at all. It's still room for forgiveness here. All I did was kiss her and that was it. I'm very young and dumb, but I'm still learning about myself"

"How could you be so damn naïve Omani?"

"Onyx I'm sorry please don't be upset with me. I don't want to lose you. I have had a lot of time to think about this and I'm ready to leave my street ties alone. I want to be with you for the long haul, I want to get my life on the right track, and I want a fresh start."

"I don't know how where going to fix this Omani?"

"Onyx hold that thought I have to go to the bathroom." Omani ran to the bathroom like she was running for the gold in a marathon. She got down on her cold knees, pushed the toilet seat up and threw up instantly. Onyx heard Omani barfing out her intestines.

"Is everything okay Omani?"

"I feel very nauseous for some reason." Omani didn't have any idea where this nausea was coming from, because she hardly ever got sick, but she sure was going to have to open up her mother eyes and prepare herself. After Omani cleaned herself up a little bit she made her way back to Onyx's bedside when Onyx's phone started ringing like a vibrator.

"Onyx your phone hasn't ringed in decades I wonder who could be calling you now?" Since Onyx's phone was closest to Omani she decided that she would answer it.

"Hello?"

"I need to speak with Onyx now so put that nigga on the phone."

"Pardon me who is this?"

"Nobody that you need to be concerned with, but I have something that I need to bring to his immediate attention and I guess your attention too since you're so damn determined to be involved."

"Whatever you have to tell him you can tell me too so spit it out!"

"Since he has a messenger now this is Tia does that name ring any bells to you?" Omani thought back to when Onyx and her were living it up in their apartment. And she remembered when Onyx brought a raggedy chick to the house named Tia.

"Oh, Tia one of Onyx's weak chicks from the club?" The whole time Onyx was just sitting there just as curious as Omani as to why Tia was calling him out of the pacific blue and what the hell she wanted.

"Whatever put me on the speaker then so both of y'all can be clear about something." Omani put the rat tailed bitch on speaker as she was directed.

"Onyx I'm 5 weeks pregnant and it's yours and I'm keeping it and ain't no way around that because you and I both know what we did and how we did it."

"What the fuck is this simple bitch talking about Onyx?"

"It takes a simple bitch to know a simple bitch Omani Sade Mitchell."

"This bitch must be high off of something because we didn't do a damn thing pregnancy related. That bitch gave me some head and that was it." Onyx was lying like a cold-hearted criminal but it wasn't like Omani wasn't going to believe him over an irrelevant bitch.

"How and why is this bitch stating my whole government name?"

"In the meantime I'm going to make sure I stay healthy and take care of this baby I'm carrying. You two go ahead and argue and I'll be in touch." Tia ended the conversation satisfied that she could cause tension in Omani's and Onyx's relationship. *I got you back bitch for the day you tried to show-out on me was all that Tia was thinking in her pregnant mind. I'm so happy I met him that night and I fucked him without a condom.* Tia wasn't on to nothing either. Her store brought clear blue stick and her OBGYN confirmations said PREGNANT. And the last person that she slept with was Onyx. It might have been just a one night stand, but that one night stand wasn't just a faded memory now. It was the beginning of motherhood for her, and she was going to enjoy every single moment of it for life.

Chapter 17:

Before I Self-Destruct

Real Men Self-Destruct, And Little Boys Go Haywire Killing Humanity...

Passive was wrapped up in extension cords like she was being apprehended by some type of federal capturing squad who was going to torture every fiber in her body. How a woman so graciously beautiful could possibly be about to suffer so much pain was baffling. Captured or not someone of Passive's rank should still be treated like royalty. She should've been wrapped up in gold, silver, or bronze chains at least. Passive hadn't ate anything since she been captured, still had that same black pillowcase draped over her face, was lying face down on a unknown mattress with no sheets, and was stripped down to her black laced bra and black laced thong panties as if someone was planning to sexually destruct her. Whatever the case was she wanted to know who the genius was behind this shady enterprise. And just when Passive was at the height of her curiosity, the orchestrators let themselves be known.

"For so long we've been living in your shadow Passive," Champagne interfered with Passive's thoughts. Champagne was supposed to be one of Smoke's and Passive's loyal drug connects, but every tree has a bad apple.

"Are you speaking for yourself or are you speaking for you and Paradise?"

"I'm speaking for all the women out here who are in the drug game. Thank you for paving the way Passive for me and Paradise, but at this point in the game its only room for one of us. My team or your team and of course I chose my team."

"So where's Paradise?"

"Don't worry about where Paradise is where is Smoke's sexy ass? I would love to give him a piece of my volcanic walls."

"If you touch my husband I promise you will never breathe again." Champagne took her whip and struck Passive on her back right across her tiger tattoo one solid time. Passive slowly arched her back in thrashing pain feeling striking skin sensations that she never felt before.

"You better watch your threats or I'm going to let this whip make an example out of you."

"Wouldn't be the first time someone tried me. Captured or not my attitude is not going to change."

"Pow!" Champagne relinquished her evil whip once again cutting Passive's gorgeous skin.

"Regardless of what you think let me tell you how this is going to go.

Smoke is going to come here to find you and when he does I'm going to kill two birds in one stone. You got to die and after I fuck him passionately he got to die too so y'all can die together."

"When he does come for me and we escape I'm going to kill you with that whip."

"Pow! Pow! Pow!" Champagne let off three hard strokes ripping into the tender skin of Passive's back. And Passive's took her pain like a champ. Not one single tear fell from her closed eyes, or one whimper came from her closed mouth. She just laid there plotting and anticipating her black knight's brisk arrival.

Even though Champagne was running things, she was still intimidated by Passive because she knew that Passive was by far a stronger woman then Champagne was and ever would be. Jealousy broiled through Champagne's antsy veins. She wanted to be a female boss so bad that she couldn't handle the title that she was trying to wear. Feeling bossy Champagne decided to call Smoke and give him head-ups on what was going on so Champagne could pull her two desperate triggers and her nerves could go back to normal.

"Ring, Ring." Smoke answered his phone on the second ring.

"Champagne I was just thinking about calling you."

"Well since I beat you to the punch I got your wife and I got your drugs so you got until sundown to come get her before I kill her and drop her dead body on your front porch like postal mail."

"Bitch I'm coming for your head and everybody else's involved with this!" Instantly Champagne hung up.

Never had Smoke related to so many females as bitches in his whole entire life, or did he have to resort to so much killing, but he was willing to do whatever it took to get Passive back in his eager arms, and he wasn't going to show any mercy to anyone. Smoke had links all over the United States including family and his links in Missouri was going to put his plan in action. Now that he knew where Passive is and who she was with he could finally concentrate on getting her back. The only thing that Smoke was happy about was that somebody else got to Passive before Lindsay did. He knew he was going to get her back, and it was only a matter of hours now, before Champagne's quiet block became a warzone.

Smoke pulled over to get himself together, and in the process of recuperating he made a couple of short calls and he got Champagne's whole network laid out for him on a silver platter, and he managed to put a few of his true loyal soldiers in place until he got there. Champagne and her team did business out of the same house that they lived in which was typical of entry-level drug dealers. Even the dumbest drug dealers know you never sleep and work in the same house. Clearly Champagne was not boss status and wasn't cutout for this game at all.

Two of Smoke's soldiers lived 20 minutes away from where Champagne resided on the west side of Missouri. Grant and Chill were Smoke's trigger happy cousins who loved killing, and loved killing for Smoke. When Grant and Chill were younger they lost their father, and the only father figure they had was Smoke. He always made sure they had a warm place to lay their heads, they had bread on the table, and money on the floor.

Smoke wasn't around long enough to stop Grant and Chill from getting mixed up in gang and gun violence so when Smoke found out that his two cousins were the most wanted gun carriers in Missouri he decided to take them under his wings. He told them if they killed for him and him only then he would honor them for the rest of their lives. Since this was a low-key way for Grant and Chill to keep them out of the public eye and still do what they loved to do so much from a man they respected and trusted they agreed.

Grant and Chill got suited up and booted up, and put their killer swag on. Guns were loaded, anticipation was heavy, and all signs were good to go. Pulling off in a black Dodge Charger, Grant and Chill were about to put the pedal to the medal because Passive was somebody that they adored dearly too, and they too would do anything and everything to get her back to Smoke. They made their way to 2906 Salisbury Street, bypassing stop signs, hitting corners, and running red lights with no problems and no regrets. Once they hit the block before Salisbury Street they found somewhere undercover to park, drew their guns, put on their masks, and jogged up the street. The two vans that Champagne used to capture Passive were parked outside her home, and so was Passive's little empty Lexus. They scoped out the premises very extensively and when they made their way to the vans to wipeout any possible occupants they found those too be empty so they decided they would take their chances and knock on Champagne's door to see exactly who was home. Before they knew it a front door was squeaking open wide.

"Who the fuck is it and what do you want?" Champagne hollered.

"Was sup Champagne?" Before Champagne even looked out her hood little security hole she opened up her door and at that point Grant and Chill bogarted their way past her slamming and locking her wooden door behind her. Grant man handled her while Chill checked the house to make sure it was clear. And since Grant didn't hear any gunshots and Chill was back in no time it was apparent that the house was now secured via them.

"Where the fuck is everybody at Champagne?"

"Up your ass and around the corner," Grant popped her to the left side of her face with his silver platted pistol.

"No they not bitch. I believe they left your ass to rot by your damn self. And they probably have gone out of town to sell the work why you try to be the independent, big, bad boss."

"So what just go ahead and kill me."

"Bitch suck my gun first." Grant took his gun and inserted into Champagne's mouth like a penis.

"And you better suck it like this was the best dick you ever had." So Champagne did as she was told to spare her wretched life. She was swallowing and deep-throating his gun up and down her wide ass throat.

"Bitch you nasty." Chill left the Champagne and Grant antics to go find Passive and remove her from the house if she agreed. The last room on the left was the room where Passive was being held. Chill couldn't believe how he found her. Back all ate up by a whip, hands tied, ankles tied by telephone extension cords, and face covered up with a pillowcase, and practically naked like somebody was going to sexually destruct her if they didn't so Chill freed Passive of all her bondages and gave her his jacket so she could cover herself up.

"Chill I'm so happy to see you, but where the hell is Smoke?"

"Smoke hasn't made it here yet, but he's aware of everything. You already know he's in route, but you know when he found out what was going on he had to get you safe ASAP."

"The sad thing about everything is this is not the end of our problems."

"Everything is good now, and it always was. I know you knew this stupid bitch wasn't going to get away with anything."

"Yeah I know so where is she?"

"Grant is handling her right now. You must have a couple blows you want to throw?"

"No I told that bitch when I escaped I was going to kill her with her own whip and that's exactly what I'm about to do." Passive found Champagne's whip and she whipped Champagne with ten long, hard, slave master strokes after Grant tied her up the exact same way that Passive was tied up. Only Champagne cried out for mercy, but Passive didn't hear anything, and didn't care if Champagne would offer her a million dollars to spare her life. Her life was gone, and Champagne fucked with the wrong bitch and she was going to make an illustration out of Champagne. Her first and probably not the last illustration of what top flight bitch not to fuck with ever in the game. Passive snatched one of Grant's guns before he could even notice that it was gone, she pulled the trigger, and shot Champagne square straight in the middle of her head like she was a pro. Grant and Chill knew that Passive was a down ass bitch, but they didn't know that she was about that life like she just portrayed herself to be. Passive was definitely not a bitch to fuck with and a bitch or a nigga would think twice before anybody tested her again in the future.

"Damn Passive I didn't know you had that in you," Grant stated shockingly.

"Never underestimate the power of a woman."

"I never will underestimate that, but let's get out of here before anybody else comes here and discovers us. And we need to hurry up and let Smoke know that you're okay." So out of Champagne's treacherous house they went back to salvation. Passive had never been so happy to walk on her own two feet and breathe ever before. Soon as Grant and Hill hit their Charger, Grant handed Passive his phone so she could call Smoke, but Passive's steady heartbeat was disrupted by his voicemail. Now her sporadic heartbeat was all over the place again because she kept redialing him and his phone kept going to voicemail. Smoke's phone rarely ever went to voicemail except for when he was about to kill, but since Passive already killed her closest wrongdoer who was Smoke going to kill now?"

"How could Smoke let his phone go to voicemail at a time like this?" Passive asked Grant as they headed for Grant and Chill's residence.

"His phone is probably dead don't trip Passive."

"His phone only goes to voicemail when he's about to kill so enlighten me on who he plans on killing."

"The only person that we knew that Smoke was going to kill today was Champagne and that's real talk Passive." All I know is my husband got sixty minutes to contact me or else

Missouri and Lindsay Chambers will just have to find out.

Still Passive kept dialing and re-dialing insistent on getting an answer from her husband. And finally she got the phone to ring. Little did she know that she was about to deal with the roughest realization that she would ever have to face in her entire empty life.

Passive was greeted by an unknown voice that was about to send Antarctica chills through her whole body.

"Hi Passive finally I have the pleasure of speaking to you personally," a shady female voice confirmed.

"Who the fuck is this and what do you mean finally?"

"I am the great Lindsay Chambers, and I'm sorry that Smoke can't come to the phone now, but you can leave a brief message though."

"Let Smoke go take me instead."

"Aren't y'all the perfect Romeo and Juliet duo? Clearly I never let him go in the first place and I'm not going to let him go."

"This doesn't have to end like this Lindsay I know he is what you have wanted all along."

"It does have to end like this. He left me all alone for you. I was supposed to be Mrs. Mitchell not you. Smoke was supposed to marry me, and trust me he will marry me now that I have him all to myself."

"Why couldn't you just find somebody else Lindsay I'm sure that you're an amazing woman," Passive tried to butter her up.

"No I couldn't and I never looked. Look for what? We both know that men like Smoke are one in a trillion so you tell me why you couldn't just bite the bait and find somebody else. I tried to get you to hook up with Omani, I tried to get you to hook up with June, but you just wouldn't fold. And I would've been satisfied if Smoke would've started messing with Shania, but that didn't work either. Always remember from this day forward if you want anything done you have to do it your damn self because you are the only person who will never let yourself down.

"So are you telling me that I have to let my husband go just like that?"

"You can search for him all you want, but I promise you will never find him. And I have already started making him forget all about you."

"Just like you didn't let him go, I'm not going to let him go so you go ahead and enjoy him while you can, but I promise you I will find him, and I will find you and when I do I'm going to handle you with a silver bullet."

Soon as Passive finished her statement Smoke's phone died. Fuck being captured; this was worst then being captured, whipped, or killed. Someone had got to Smoke before Smoke could get to Passive. And now the tables were turnt once again, and the tables weren't turnt in Passive's favor. She was definitely about to prepare herself to make Another Shady Mission, because now she had to be superwoman, and now she had to be in charge, and now she had to save her husband from his shady ex-girlfriend. Whether it was going to take days, weeks, months, or years, no amount of time was going to be time-consuming for her. She was never going to stop making shady missions now and she was going to find Darnell "Smoke" Mitchell and bring him back in one peace. If anyone tried to stop her, or get in her way she was going to kill them without any hesitations, and she was going to kill until she found her first true love. Passive was never a shady person beforehand, but now she understood why people became shady. If only she would've told Smoke everything the moment it happened, then maybe Passive wouldn't be in this cold predicament right now feeling like a black widow. *Bitches are just mad because they know they ain't no competition to me, but I'm still Passive Boone Mitchell, and I wasn't given this name for no reason. I didn't become a drug transporter for no reason, and I didn't make wedding vows for no reason so I'll see you in a minute bitch. It's been real, but Another Shady Mission is coming so you better be ready because this time Passive is going to be the .22 millimeter problem-solver, the prosperous don-diva, and the baddest H.B.I.C to ever hit the drug game.*

The Shady Escapes are To Be
Continued…

www.ingramcontent.com/pod-product-compliance
Lightning Source LLC
Chambersburg PA
CBHW071134170626

46809CB00002B/609